"As Part Of The Deal, You And I Will Continue The Affair We Started A Month Ago."

Her jaw dropped in shock. "You're joking, aren't you?"

"I told you there would be a cost. Can you honestly tell me that you didn't enjoy that night we shared?"

Her cheeks turned pink with the color that damned her protest.

"You and I have a lot in common," he said. "And it translates physically. I can give you something you need and you give me something I want." He wouldn't use the word *need*. He would never be that vulnerable.

"So, you're buying me," she whispered.

"The drama isn't necessary," he said in a dry voice. "I want you. If you'll admit it, you want me, too. I can give you things you need, but I want something in return. What's wrong with that?"

She closed her eyes, her dark eyelashes providing a fan of mystery. One. Two. Three seconds later, she opened her eyes and stared at him. "What's wrong with that? Just everything."

Dear Reader,

Happy Valentine's Day! I'm sending you something better than chocolate—powerful and hot Michael Medici!

The Playboy's Proposition features sexy, self-made workaholic Michael of THE MEDICI MEN. Michael is accustomed to getting what he wants, and he wants Bella St. Clair.

Despite their strength and resilience, both suffer pain and secret guilt and would do anything to make things right for their loved ones. Michael doesn't understand his deeper than bone-deep attraction to Bella. And Bella doesn't trust Michael with her broken heart.

What they have to learn is how to deal with the unexpected, amazing experience of finding their soul mates. As you, dear reader, already know, a soul mate is that special person who loves you, heals you and inspires you to be the best person you can be. And you do the same for them!

Please drop me a line if you get a chance to read Michael and Bella's story. I would love to hear from you at leanne@leannebanks.com

Wishing you all the best in love and life,

Leanne Banks

LEANNE BANKS

THE PLAYBOY'S PROPOSITION

Published by Silhouette Books
America's Publisher of Contemporary Romance

 SILHOUETTE BOOKS

Recycling programs
for this product may
not exist in your area.

ISBN-13: 978-0-373-73008-7

THE PLAYBOY'S PROPOSITION

Visit Silhouette Books at www.eHarlequin.com

Printed in U.S.A.

Books by Leanne Banks

Silhouette Desire

Royal Dad #1400
Tall, Dark & Royal #1412
**His Majesty, M.D.* #1435
The Playboy & Plain Jane #1483
**Princess in His Bed* #1515
Between Duty and Desire #1599
Shocking the Senator #1621
Billionaire's Proposition #1699
†*Bedded by the Billionaire* #1863
†*Billionaire's Marriage Bargain* #1886
Blackmailed Into a Fake Engagement #1916
†*Billionaire Extraordinaire* #1939
**From Playboy to Papa!* #1987
**The Playboy's Proposition* #1995

*The Royal Dumonts
†The Billionaires Club
**The Medici Men

LEANNE BANKS

is a *New York Times* and *USA TODAY* bestselling author who is surprised every time she realizes how many books she has written. Leanne loves chocolate, the beach and new adventures. To name a few, Leanne has ridden on an elephant, stood on an ostrich egg (no, it didn't break), gone parasailing and indoor skydiving. Leanne loves writing romance because she believes in the power and magic of love. She lives in Virginia with her family and four-and-a-half-pound Pomeranian named Bijou. Visit her Web site at www.leannebanks.com.

This book is dedicated to the BBs. Thank you for providing me with never-ending inspiration. Catherine Baker, Peggy Blake, Coco Carruth, Ann Cholewinski, Rose Dunn, Kim Jones, Mina McAllister, Sharon Neblett, Terry Parker, Terri Shea, Sandy Smith, Kathy Venable, Jane Wargo, Kathy Zaremba.

Prologue

Mr. Always-Pays-Cash-And-Tips-Well. Bella St. Clair spotted the hot, sophisticated dark-haired customer in the back corner of the packed Atlanta bar. He'd been there four of the ten nights she'd worked at Monahan's. Always polite, he'd chatted with her a few times, making her feel like a person instead of just a cocktail waitress. Despite the fact that in terms of romance her heart was deader than a doornail, and she was distracted about her aunt's latest problem, Bella felt a fraction of her misery fade at the sight of him.

He gave a slight nod and she moved toward him. "Good evening. How are you tonight?" she asked, setting a paper napkin on the table.

He hesitated a half beat then shrugged. "I've had better," he said.

A shot of empathy twisted through her. She could

identify with him. Her aunt's business had been turned over to the bank one month ago today and Bella knew it was at least partly her fault. "Sorry," she said. "Maybe the atmosphere here will distract you. A jazz artist will be playing in a little while. What can I get for you?"

"Maclellan single malt whiskey," he said.

She lifted her eyebrows at the expensive beverage and nodded. "Excellent choice for either a rough night or a celebration. Can I get you anything to eat with that?"

"No thanks. Rowdy crowd tonight," he said, nodding toward the large table in the center of the room. "Must be the snow."

She glanced toward the curtained windows in dismay. "I've been so busy since I arrived that I didn't notice. I heard the forecast, but it's rare to get the white stuff here. Think it'll be just a dusting?" she asked hopefully.

He shook his head. "We're already past a dusting. The roads should be covered in an hour."

"Great," she muttered. "My little car is gonna love this trip home."

"What do you drive?" he asked, curiosity glinting in his dark eyes.

"Volkswagen Beetle."

He chuckled. "I guess that's better than a motorcycle."

She felt a bubble of gallows amusement. "Thanks for the encouragement. I'll be right back with your whiskey." She got his drink from the bartender and made her way through the crowd, carefully balancing the glass of whiskey on her tray. Heaven knew, she didn't want to spill a drop. The stuff cost fifty bucks a shot.

She wondered what had caused her handsome customer the pain she glimpsed in his dark eyes. He emanated confidence and a kind of dynamic electricity that snapped her out of the twilight zone she'd been in for the last month.

She set the glass in front of him. "There you go," she said, meeting his dark gaze and feeling a surprising sizzle. She blinked. Where had that come from? She'd thought all her opportunities for sizzle had passed her by.

She watched him lift the glass to his lips and take a sip. The movement drew her attention to his mouth, sensual and firm. She felt a burning sensation on her own lips, surprised again at her reaction.

"Thanks," he said.

She nodded, transfixed.

"Hey babe," a voice called from behind her. "We want another round."

The call pulled her out of her temporary daze. "Oops. Gotta go. Do you need anything else?"

"Water when you get a chance," he said. "Thank you very much, Bella," he said in a voice that made her stomach dip.

She turned around, wishing she knew his name. "Wow," she whispered to herself. Based on her reaction to the man, one would almost think she was the one drinking whiskey. *Crazy*, she thought, and returned to the rest of her customers.

Another dead end. Sometimes it seemed his life's curse was to never find his brother. Too restless to suffer the stark silence in his luxury home, Michael Medici settled back in his seat in a corner of the crowded popular bar, one of several he owned in Atlanta.

Michael usually craved quiet at the end of the day, but tonight was different. The din of Atlanta's young crowd buffeted the frustration and pain rolling inside him.

Michael spent the next hour allowing himself the luxury of watching Bella. After the disappointing news from the private investigator, he craved a distraction. He wondered if he would ever find out what had truly happened to his brother all those years ago. Or if he was cursed to stay in limbo for the rest of his life.

Forcing his mind away from his frustration, he watched Bella, enjoying the way she bit her pink mouth when she met his gaze. Feeling the arousal build between them, he toyed with the idea of taking her home with him. Some might consider that arrogant, given he'd just met her recently, but Michael usually got what he wanted from business and the opposite sex.

He slid his gaze over her curvy body. Her uniform, consisting of a white blouse, black skirt and tights, revealed rounded breasts, a narrow waist and inviting hips. Her legs weren't bad, either.

She set another glass of water on his table.

"How are you liking it here?" he asked.

She hesitated and met his gaze. "It's good so far. I've been out of the country for a year. I'm re-acclimating to being an average American again."

"You don't look average to me," he said. "What were you doing out of the country if you don't mind my asking?"

"Disaster relief."

"Ah," he said with a nod. A do-gooder. Perhaps that accounted for her other-worldly aura. "How's the transition going?"

"Bumpy," she said with a smile that made him feel like he'd been kicked in his gut.

He didn't make a habit of picking up cocktail wait-resses, especially those who worked for businesses he owned, but this one intrigued him. He wondered if she was the kind of woman who would be impressed by his wealth. Just for fun, he decided to keep his identity a secret a little longer. He liked the idea of not dealing with dollar signs in a woman's eyes. He'd been featured in the Atlanta magazine often enough that he could rarely meet someone without them knowing way too much about him. Way too much about his business success, anyway.

"I don't see a ring on your finger, Bella," he said.

Her eyes showed a trace of sadness. "That's right. You don't."

"Would you like me to give you a ride home? I think my SUV may be better able to take on a snowy road."

Her eyes widened slightly in surprise and he watched her pause in a millisecond of indecision. "I'm not supposed to fraternize with the customers."

"Once we step outside the door, I won't be one any longer," he said, familiar with the policy.

She looked both tempted and reluctant. "I don't even know your name."

"Michael. I'll hang around awhile longer," he said, amused that she'd almost turned him down. He tried to remember the last time that had happened.

Watching her from his corner, he noticed a man reaching toward her. She backed away and the man stood. Michael narrowed his eyes.

The man reached for her and pulled her against him. "Come on baby, you're so hot. And it's cold outside…" The man slid his hand down toward her bottom.

Already on his feet, Michael walked toward Bella

and pushed the man aside and into a chair. "I think you've had too much." Glancing around the room, he saw the bar manager, Jim, and gave a quick curt nod.

Seconds later, Jim arrived, stumbling over his words. "I'll take care of this Mr.—"

Michael gave another curt nod, cutting the man off mid-sentence. "Thank you. Perhaps your staff needs a break."

Jim nodded. "Take the rest of the night off," the manager said.

Her face pale, Bella hesitated. "I—"

"I'll give you a ride whenever you want to go," Michael said. "I can take you somewhere quieter."

She met his gaze and he saw a glimmer of trust in her eyes as if she felt the same strange sense of connection with him he did with her. She paused a halfbeat, then nodded. "Okay."

An hour and a half later, Bella realized she'd told half her life story to the hot man who'd rescued her at work. She'd told him about how her Aunt Charlotte had raised her. She'd even vaguely mentioned being a failure at her love life. Every time she thought about Stephen, a stab of loss wrenched through her. She knew she would never get over him. Never. The worst though, was her crushing guilt over not being with her aunt while she suffered through the cancer treatment.

Although she hadn't mentioned any names, she was appalled at how much she'd revealed. "I've done all the talking," she said, covering her face. "And I can't even blame it on alcohol because, except for that first man-gotini, I've been drinking water. You heard enough about me a long time ago. Your turn. Tell me why this has been a rotten day for you."

"I can't agree about hearing enough about you," he said with a half smile playing over his beautiful mouth. It occurred to Bella that his mouth, his face, should have been carved in marble and exhibited in a museum. She glanced at his broad shoulders and fit body. *Perhaps his body, too,* she thought.

"You're very kind," she said. "But it's still your turn."

He gave a low chuckle, his dark eyes mysterious. "Not many people have described me as kind. But if you insist," he said, lifting his own glass of water to take a drink.

"I do," she said.

"My parents died when I was young, so I wasn't raised by them. You and I share that in common."

"Who did raise you?" she asked.

"I wasn't lucky enough to have an Aunt Charlotte," he said. "No need for sympathy," he said.

"Oh," she said, studying his face. He was an interesting combination of strength and practicality. "That must have been hard, though."

"It was," he nodded and paused a moment. "The accident tore my family apart."

"That's horrible," she said, filled with questions.

"It was," he agreed. "I keep wondering if I could have done something…"

Silence followed, and Bella felt a well of understanding build inside her. The force of the emotion should have surprised her, but she identified with the depth of his misery all too easily. She slid her hand over his. "You feel guilty, don't you?"

He glanced down at her hand on his. "Every day," he said. He broke off. "It's probably just a wish…"

Her heart twisted inside her. "I understand," she whispered.

He rubbed his thumb over her hand. "You're not just beautiful. You're intuitive," he said.

Bella wouldn't have called herself beautiful. In fact, she couldn't remember anyone doing so except Stephen. Her stomach knotted at the memory. He would never call her beautiful again, now that he'd fallen in love with someone else.

"There you go again, being too kind," she said.

"You have that confused. I suspect you're the kind one. I can't believe you don't have to turn away men all the time."

"Now that's flattery," she said. "Unless you're counting the ones who've had too much to drink at the bar." She knew she was unusual looking. The contrast of her dark hair, intense eyes and pale skin sometimes drew second glances, but she suspected they were more due to curiosity than admiration.

"I'd like to spend more time with you," he said, his eyes dark with seduction.

Her heart, which she'd thought was dead, tripped over itself. Bella reminded herself that her heart raced for many reasons, fear, excitement, inexplicable arousal…

"I'm not in the best place emotionally for any sort of relationship."

"I wasn't suggesting anything serious," he said. "The only thing we need to take seriously is each other's pleasure."

Her breath caught at the sensual expression on his face. "A one-night stand?" she said, surprised she wasn't immediately rejecting the offer. Heaven knew, she'd never accepted such a proposition before. That had been before she'd fallen in love and lost her heart. That had been before she'd had her chance and saw it slip away. Michael wasn't suggesting anything like that. She felt a surprising twinge of relief.

"It depends on what we want after the night is over. You and I have some things in common. I could make you forget your problems for awhile. I think you could do the same for me."

The lure was too tempting. He was strong, but she'd glimpsed his humanity and for some reason there was a strange connection between them. A connection that made her feel a little more alive than like the walking dead.

She took a sip to moisten her suddenly dry throat. Was she really going to do this? "I don't even know your last name," she said.

"Michael Medici," he said with a slight smile. "You can run a background check, but you won't find anything on me. We'd also be wasting time. If you need someone to vouch for me, you can call your boss. He knows me."

One

Bella awakened to the sensation of being covered in the softest, finest cotton sheets…and wrapped in the strong, but unfamiliar arms of the man who'd made love to her most of the night.

Her chest tightened into a hard knot at the realization that she'd slept with a near stranger. What had possessed her? Was it because she still hadn't recovered from her breakup with her ex-fiancé? Was it because she needed to escape the guilt she felt for not being there for her aunt when she'd needed her most?

She blinked her bleary eyes several times then closed them again. It had been so easy to accept Michael Medici's offer to drive her home in the rare Atlanta snowstorm with a stop at a cozy bar. Somehow, she'd ended up in his bed instead.

Taking a quick breath, she felt the overwhelming need

to run. This had been a huge mistake. She wasn't that kind of woman. Scooting a millimeter at a time, she got to the side of the bed and gently slid her foot to the ground.

"Where are you going?" Michael asked, causing her to stop midmotion.

She glanced over her shoulder and the sight of him covered by a sheet only from the waist down made her throat tighten. In the soft darkness before dawn, he leaned against one forearm, and his broad shoulders and muscular chest emanated strength. She forced herself to meet his gaze and saw what had attracted her from the beginning—dark eyes that glowed with confidence and attentiveness. She'd pushed her fingers through his dark curly hair. His mouth had taken her with shocking passion.

She cleared her throat and tried to clear her mind. "I realized I have a job interview today. I should get home."

"You don't think the interview will be canceled due to the snowstorm?" he asked.

"Well, I can't be sure," she said a bit too brightly for her own ears. "Always best to be prepared. You don't have to get up. I'll call a cab."

He gave a short laugh and rose from the bed. "Fat chance in this weather. I'll take you."

She looked away. "Oh, no really—"

"I insist," he said in a rock-solid tone.

"But my car," she said.

"I'll have my driver bring it to your place."

One hour later, Michael turned into her apartment complex. Bella let out a tiny breath of relief in anticipation of escaping such close confines with him. During the silent ride, she'd spent every other minute castigating herself for making such a foolish choice. She needed to step up and be there for her aunt. She refused to be like her mother—irresponsible and careless of others' needs.

"Is this the building?" Michael asked.

"Yes," she said, her hand on the door as he pulled to a stop. "I really appreciate the ride home. It was very kind of you."

"I'd like to see you again," he said, and something in his voice forced her to meet his gaze.

If she were another person, if she had fewer responsibilities, if she weren't still in love with a man she couldn't have…too many ifs.

She shook her head. "It's not a good idea. I shouldn't have—" She broke off and cleared her throat. Lord, this was awkward.

He leaned toward her. "You didn't like being in my bed?" he asked, but it was more of a dare than a question.

She sucked in a quick breath. "I didn't say that. I just have a lot going on right now. I think being with you could be confusing for me."

"It doesn't have to be confusing," he said. "It's simple. I meet your needs and you meet mine."

She couldn't stop a bubble of nervous laughter as she looked into his dark gaze. How could anything with this man ever be simple? She was out of her league and she knew it. "I—uh—I don't think so." She shook her head. "Thank you for bringing me home."

Bella raced inside her apartment and closed the door behind her. She took several deep breaths, still unable to believe that she had spent the night with a man she barely knew.

She checked the time. A little too early for her regular morning call with Aunt Charlotte. She took a shower and let the hot spray rinse away her stress and warm her from the outside in. For a few minutes, she forgot about her worries and focused on the warm water.

After she got out of the shower, she dried off, dressed and checked the time again. She dialed her aunt's number and waited while it rang several times. Bella felt her concern grow the longer it took for Charlotte to answer.

Bella had almost lost her and she still could. Her aunt was recovering from breast cancer and a year of grueling treatment, a year when Bella had been away pursuing her dream. If only Charlotte hadn't kept her illness a secret.

"Hello," her aunt said in a sleepy voice.

"Oh, no, I woke you," Bella said.

"No," Charlotte said and sighed. "Well, actually you did. The shop is closed today."

"So you get a day off," Bella said, excited at the prospect of her aunt getting some extra rest.

"Without pay," Charlotte grumbled.

"Can I bring something over for you? Soup, sandwich, coffee, green tea…"

"Don't you dare," Charlotte said. "I don't want you driving in this messy weather. I have plenty of food here. Maybe I'll do something really decadent and stay in bed and watch the morning shows."

"As long as you promise to eat something," Bella said.

"You sound just like a mom," Charlotte said.

"I want to make up for lost time."

"Oh, sweetie," her aunt said. "You gotta let go of that. I made it through."

"But you lost something important to you," Bella said, speaking of her aunt's spa. It had been her aunt's life-long dream to open several spas in Atlanta and Charlotte had succeeded until the disease and treatment had sucked the energy out of her.

"True, but things could be worse." She laughed. "My hair is growing back. I'm thinking of dying it pink."

Bella smiled. "Or purple?"

"Yeah," Charlotte said. "Speaking of spas, I found out who bought the business from the bank."

"Really? How did you find out?"

"A client who came into the salon works for the bank. She said some local big wheeler and dealer bought them. She said he's known for buying and selling bankrupt businesses."

Bella made a face. The man she described sounded like a vulture. "Not exactly Prince Charming," she muttered.

"I don't know," her aunt said. "The client said if there were a picture in the dictionary beside the word *hot*, this guy would be right there. I haven't heard of him, but apparently he's well known among local businesses. Michael Medici's his name."

Two

Three weeks later, Bella walked into MM Enterprises mustering the fragile hope that Michael Medici would show an ounce of compassion for her Aunt Charlotte. She knew the deck was stacked against her in more ways than one, but she had to try. In an ironic twist of fate, Michael's company had bought her aunt's business before Bella had even met him. Apparently, Michael was known for scooping up the skeletons of failing companies and either breathing new life into them, or partitioning them into smaller pieces and making a profit.

The heels of her boots clicked against the tile floor. Dressed in black from head to toe, she could have been outfitted for a funeral. Instead, she was dressing for success. More than anything, she needed Michael to take her seriously. Stepping into the elevator, her nerves jumped under her skin, and she mentally rehearsed her request for the millionth time. The elevator dinged, signaling its arrival. She walked down the hallway and took a breath just before she opened the door to his office.

A young woman seated behind a desk wearing a Bluetooth glanced up in inquiry. "May I help you?"

"I'm Bella St. Clair. I have an appointment with Mr. Medici," she said.

The receptionist nodded. "Please take a seat. He'll be right with you."

Bella sat on the edge of the upholstered blue chair and unbuttoned her coat as she glanced around the office. Business magazines were fanned out neatly on top of the cherry sofa table. Mirrors and original artwork graced cream-colored walls and a large aquarium filled with colorful fish caught her attention. She wondered if any of those fish were from the shark family. She wondered if Michael would ultimately be ruthless or reasonable.

She resisted the urge to fidget. Barely. This was her chance to make it up to Charlotte for not being there when her aunt had needed her most.

Her heart still wrenched at what Charlotte had suffered. Charlotte had supported Bella while she pursued her dream of taking a year off to work for disaster relief in Europe, and had kept her diagnosis a secret from Bella until she'd arrived back in the States.

"You can go in now," the receptionist said, jolting Bella back from her reverie.

Stiffening her spine, she stood and smiled at the receptionist. "Thank you," she said and hesitated a half beat before she opened the door to Michael Medici's office.

Walking inside, she saw him standing in front of the wall of windows on the opposite wall. The sight of him hit her like a strike to her gut. His dark, commanding frame provided a stark contrast against the blue sky behind him. His eyes seemed colder than the last time she'd seen him.

She bit the inside of her cheek. Why shouldn't he be cold toward her? She'd rejected his suggestion that they continue their affair. She was lucky he was willing to see her at all. That had been her litmus test. If he would talk to her, then maybe she could persuade him to agree to her proposal.

"Bella," he said in the smooth velvety voice she remembered. "What brings you here?"

Step one. Address the past and move on. "I realize that you and I shared a rather unusual experience a few weeks ago," she began.

"On the contrary," he said with a slight mocking glint in his eyes. "I understand it happens every day, all over the world."

Her cheeks burned at the remembered intimacy. "Not quite the way that—" She gave up and cleared her throat. "That night aside, I would like to discuss a business proposition with you."

He lifted an eyebrow in surprise and moved to the front of his desk, sitting on the edge. "A business proposition? Have a seat," he said, waving his hand to one of the leather chairs in front of him.

Moving closer to him to sit down, she caught a whiff of his cologne. A hot visual of him naked in bed with her seared her memory. His proximity jangled her nerves, but she was determined. "There's a lot that you and I don't know about each other, but I did tell you that my

Aunt Charlotte had experienced some health problems and was also having a tough time professionally."

He nodded silently.

She had wished that he would be less handsome than the last time she'd seen him. Her wish had not come true. She took another breath, wanting to clear her head. "What I didn't tell you was that while I was out of the country last year, my aunt was diagnosed with cancer. She hid that from me or I would have come back immediately. She had to undergo treatment that weakened her. She's better now, but she wasn't able to focus on her business during that time. She lost it."

"I'm sorry to hear that," he said.

"Thank you," she said, feeling a sliver of relief at his words of compassion. "This has been so hard on my aunt. She's sinking into a depression over it. I did some research and found out that you bought her business from the bank."

He tilted his head to one side, frowning. "What business?"

"The spas," she said. "Charlotte's Day Spas."

Realization crossed his face. "Right. She had three of them. I'm planning to convert the properties and resell them. One is a perfect location for a pizza franchise."

"Pizza," she echoed, dismayed at the thought. She cleared her throat. "What I would like to propose is to arrange a loan with you for us to buy back the businesses with the agreement that you would get a share of the profit."

He looked at her for a long moment. "Which at the moment is zero," he said.

"It obviously won't stay that way. The only reason the spas crashed was because of my aunt's health problems."

"And what do you plan to use to secure the loan?" he asked.

"We don't have anything tangible, but the important thing is that my aunt and I would be willing to work night and day to make this work."

"Do you really think, with her health, she can work night and day?" he asked.

She bit her lip. "She needs a purpose. She feels as if she's lost everything." She sighed. "No. I wouldn't let her work night and day, but I could work that hard. I'm young. I'm strong. I can do this."

"So, you're asking me to bank on you and your commitment," he said. "Do you have a résumé?"

He was as cool as a swim in the Arctic, only revealing his thoughts when he wanted, Bella thought with a twinge of resentment. No wonder he was known for his business expertise. She thought of all the menial jobs she'd taken to help finance her education and felt a sinking sensation. She gave him the manila folder that contained the business plan and her résumé. "As you can see, I'm a licensed esthetician, and I have a bachelor's degree in communication studies."

He glanced over the paper. "If you're so committed to your aunt's spas, then why did you go to college? You had your esthetician's license."

"My aunt and I agreed that I should get a college education."

He nodded, looking through the papers. He rubbed his jaw thoughtfully with his hand. "I'll get back to you."

Michael watched Bella leave his office. *Damn her,* he whispered after she'd closed the door behind her. He hadn't stopped thinking about her since he'd had her in his bed. Since she'd rejected him after they'd made wild, passionate love.

He chuckled bitterly to himself. *Love* was a misnomer. Amazing sex was much more accurate. He'd sensed a desperation similar to his in her. She'd been so hot, he'd almost felt as if she'd singed his hands, his body....

Scowling at his reaction to her, he wondered why he wanted her so much. He usually took women as lovers then tired of them after a while. After just one night of her, he knew he had to have more. It was more than want. Need.

Not likely, he told himself, releasing the fist he'd just noticed was clenched. He needed to get her out of his system. The fact that she'd rejected him only added fuel to the fire.

He punched the intercom button for his receptionist. "Call my investigator. I want him to run a credit and background check on Charlotte Ambrose and Bella St. Clair. I want it by tomorrow." He didn't know why he was even considering Bella's request. Michael had always kept emotion out of his business decisions. That was part of the reason he was so successful. A frisson of challenge fluttered at the idea of turning Charlotte's business into a success. If success were possible, he would know how to make it happen.

His BlackBerry buzzed. He glanced at the caller ID. Rafe, his brother, a yachting business owner, lived in Miami. His mood lifting, he punched the on button. "Rafe? How are you? You must not be very busy if you're calling me." All the Medici men were work-aholics. Being farmed out to different foster homes after their parents died had left all of them with a nearly unquenchable thirst for success and control.

"On the contrary. I got married a few weeks ago, remember?" Rafe said.

"Yes. Even I was surprised you were able to pull that off. Nicole seemed very reluctant." Michael was still amazed that Rafe had persuaded the beautiful guardian of his brother's child to marry him so quickly.

"I have more news," Rafe said.

"Yes?" Michael asked, hoping Rafe had learned something new about their missing brother Leo.

"You're going to be an uncle again," Rafe told him, joy threaded through his voice. Even though he hadn't seen Leo in twenty years, Michael thought about his brother every day.

Michael felt a twinge of disappointment that the news wasn't about Leo, but he couldn't stop from smiling. "So fast?"

"Some things are meant to be," Rafe said.

"How does Nicole feel about it?"

"Besides being mildly nauseated, she's thrilled," Rafe said.

"And Joel?" Michael asked, thinking of Rafe's son.

"He doesn't know yet. We thought we'd wait until she's showing," Rafe said. "But we want you to come down to visit."

Michael shook his head. "I'm slammed at the moment. Lots of buying and selling action right now."

"Yeah?" Rafe said. "I asked an investigator to look into leads for Aunt Emilia."

"So did I," Michael said, and started to pace. Their aunt Emilia lived in Italy and had sent Rafe photos and some curious letters recently. "Nothing yet. I also had my investigator run another search on Leo."

"Nothing, right?" Rafe said.

"Right," Michael said. "I've decided to try a P.I. who lives in Philly. He's always lived in the state. Maybe a native will spot something that we can't see."

"It might be worth trying," Rafe said, but Michael could hear the skepticism in his brother's voice.

"I have to try," Michael said. "One way or another, I need to do this for Leo."

"You're going to have to give up the guilt someday," Rafe said. "You were a child when Dad and Leo took that trip on the train. You couldn't have possibly known there would be a wreck or that they would die."

"Easy to say," Michael muttered, still feeling the crushing heavy sense of responsibility tighten his chest like a vise. "It was supposed to be me. Leo went in my place. The least I can do, if he really *did* die, is give him a proper burial."

"If anyone can make it happen, you can," Rafe said.

"Thanks." Michael raked his hand through his hair.

"In the meantime, though, Damien is talking about coming for a visit. If he travels all the way from Vegas, then the least you can do is hop down here too. I'm not taking no for an answer," he said forcefully.

"Okay," Michael said. "Keep me posted."

"Will do. Take care of yourself."

Two days later, Michael told his assistant to set up another appointment for Bella. One day after that, she walked through his office door. He noticed she was dressed from head to toe in black again. She might as well have been grieving. He suspected her pride *was* in mourning.

Her eyes—a startling shade of violet—regarded him

with a combination of reticence and hope bordering on desperation.

Michael could assuage that desperation. He could make her wish come true, but Charlotte and Bella would have to do things his way. Michael had learned long ago that one of the primary reasons businesses failed was because the owners were unwilling to give up their ideas in exchange for success.

"Have a seat," he said, and leaned against his desk.

She sank on to the edge of the leather chair and lifted her chin in false bravado. He liked her all the more for that. She might very well hate him by the end of their meeting.

"There might be a way this can work, but it will cost both you and your aunt. We do it my way, or I'm out."

She bit the inside of her upper lip. He resisted the urge to tell her not to do that. Her lips were too beautiful. The pink-purple color of her bee-stung mouth provided a sensual contrast to her ivory skin. Her mouth was pure sex to him, and when she licked her lips…

"What is your way?" she asked.

"We start with one spa and do it right," he said.

"But Charlotte had three—"

"And is still recovering from chemotherapy," he said.

She took a breath and pursed her lips, her gaze sliding away from his. "Go on," she said.

"In this economy, people want luxury at a discount."

"But you have to pay for good service—"

"Yes, but people need to feel as if they aren't spending too much on splurging." He opened the file folder. "I researched the business plans of successful spas. You need to focus on what they call miniservices and discounts for volume purchases. A minifacial. Packages of massages.

A package of ten pedicures at a discount. In turn, you provide a quality service, but limit the time."

"Sounds like fast food," she said, curling her beautiful lip.

"Exactly," he said. "People can justify fast food more easily than lobster and filet mignon. Filet mignon is a commitment."

She paused and threaded her fingers through her dark hair. "I don't know if Charlotte will go for this."

"The deal is nonnegotiable," he said and felt not one qualm. Michael knew how to split the wheat from the chaff. "I'm bending my rules by offering this plan to you."

She blinked in surprise. "How are you bending your rules?"

"If someone loses their business, then they're not a good enough bet for me to give them a second try," he said in a blunt tone.

Bella's eyes widened. "Even though she got sick?"

"For whatever reason," he said. "When you're in trouble or you can't cover your responsibilities, you always make sure you have someone to cover for you. If you're not a superhero, you have to have a backup."

She met his gaze. "What about you? Who's your backup? Or are you a superhero?"

He chuckled at her audacity. "If anything unforeseen should happen to me, my attorney will step in."

"I'm sure you pay him very well," she said.

"I do."

"Not everyone has that luxury," she said.

"It's not a luxury. It's a necessity," he said. "And I'll require it as part of the business plan."

"I'm her backup," she said, lifting her chin again. "That's settled."

"In this case, I will need an additional backup," he said.

"Why?" she asked. "I'm trained and dependable and completely committed."

"I have another job for you," he said, watching her carefully. He thought about Bella far too often. The images of the night they shared together burned through his mind like a red-hot iron. Plus there was something in her eyes that clicked with him. Her effect on him was a mystery. Once he solved that mystery, he would be free.

"What?" she demanded. "I need to help my aunt. There's nothing more important."

"You'll be able to help her. I won't demand all your time," he said. "But as part of the deal, you and I will continue the affair we started a month ago."

Her jaw dropped in shock. "You're joking, aren't you?"

"I told you there would be a cost to both you and your aunt. Can you honestly tell me that you didn't enjoy that night we shared?"

Her cheeks turned pink with the color that damned her protest. She looked away.

"You and I have a lot in common," he said. "And it translates physically. I can give you something you need and you give me something I want." He wouldn't use the word need. He would never be that vulnerable.

"I would feel like a prostitute," she whispered.

"The drama isn't necessary," he said in a dry voice. "I want you. If you'll admit it, you want me, too. I can give you things you need. I can help take care of your aunt, but I want something in return. What's wrong with that?"

She closed her eyes, her dark eyelashes providing a fan of mystery. One. Two. Three seconds later, she opened her eyes and stared at him. "What's wrong with that? Everything."

Three

"Think it over," Bella muttered, repeating Michael's parting words. She was so frustrated she could scream. In fact, she had done just that in the privacy of her Volkswagen Beetle.

Spotting her favorite coffee shop, she squeezed her vehicle into a small space alongside the curb and scooted inside the shop. The scent of fresh coffee and baked goods wafted over her, making her mouth water. A half second later, she was hit with a double shot of nostalgia and pain. She and Stephen, her ex-fiancé, had spent many hours here. She glanced in the direction of their favorite booth in the corner next to the window, perfect for the times they'd spent talking about the future they would share.

The hurt she'd tried to escape slid past her defenses. During her time in Europe, Bella had not only missed out on helping her Aunt Charlotte when she'd needed her most, she'd also lost the only man she'd ever loved.

Pushing past the feeling of loss that never seemed to go away, Bella decided this was a perfect occasion for a cupcake and vanilla latte. She slid into a seat next to the window and took a bite off the top of the cupcake.

Michael had made an impossible offer. Although she had known it would be a longshot for him to give her aunt another chance with the spa business, she'd been certain he wouldn't solicit her again. Reason number one was that she'd turned him down after the night they'd shared. Reason number two was she couldn't believe he would still be that interested in her. A man like Michael could have just about any woman he wanted. So why would he want her?

She would be lying if she said she hadn't thought about the hot night they'd shared. It was branded in her memory, but she'd known it was a mistake the next morning. Her body may have responded to Michael, but she knew her heart still belonged to Stephen. Her heart would always belong to Stephen.

The stress the distance had created had just been too much. Stephen had been unbearably lonely and losing his job had been too much. She remembered the day he'd called her to tell her he hadn't intended to fall in love with someone else. His voice had broken and she could hear his remorse even from all those miles away. He'd fought it, but he'd told her he'd realized he'd needed someone who needed him as much as he needed her.

So, Bella had not only let her aunt down, she'd also let down the love of her life. A bitter taste filled her mouth. Bella had spent her lifetime determined not to be anything like her undependable mother, a woman who'd dumped her on Charlotte. Her mother had been known for disappearing during difficult times. Bella refused to be that person who couldn't be counted on, yet in one year, she'd failed to be there for the people she loved most.

Overwhelmed by the disappointment she felt in herself, she closed her eyes for a long moment and took a deep breath. There had to be a way she could still help Aunt Charlotte. Some other way....

"Bella," a familiar male voice said, and she opened her eyes. Her stomach clenched at the sight of Stephen and a lovely blond woman.

"Stephen," she said, thinking that he and the woman with him looked like a matched pair. Both had blonde hair, blue eyes. And they glowed with love. A knot of loss tightened in her throat. "It's good to see you."

He nodded then glanced at the woman beside him. "Bella, this is Britney Kensington. She is—" He seemed to falter.

The awkwardness seemed to suck the very breath from her lungs, but she was determined not to let it show. "It's nice to meet you, Britney," she said.

Britney smiled brightly, and based on her expression, Bella concluded that the woman hadn't a clue that she and Stephen had been romantically involved. "My pleasure. What Stephen was trying to say was I am his fiancée." She lifted her left hand to flash a diamond ring.

Bella felt the knife twist inside her. She'd known Stephen had fallen in love, but she hadn't known he was officially engaged. Somewhere in her heart, a door shut.

Although she'd mentally accepted that she'd lost Stephen, there must have been some small part of her that had hoped there was still a chance. This was solid proof that there was no chance for her and Stephen. No chance at all.

Bella cleared her throat. "Your ring is beautiful. Congratulations to both of you." She glanced at her watch. "Oh my goodness, I've lost track of the time. I need to run. It was good seeing you," she said and pulled on her coat. Grabbing her latte and scooping up the half-eaten cupcake, she dumped them into the trash. She wouldn't be able to choke down one more bite.

"Bella," Stephen said, his handsome face creased in concern. "How is your aunt?"

"Growing stronger every day," she said. "She's completed her treatment and everything looks good."

"Please tell her I send my best," he said.

"Thank you. I'll do that. Bye now," she said, and forced her lips into a pleasant smile before she walked out of the coffee shop.

Bella spent the afternoon waitressing at the restaurant. Despite the popularity of the place, the lunch crowd had been light, giving her too much of an opportunity to brood over her aunt's situation.

After work, she picked up a take-out meal of chicken soup and a club sandwich to take to Charlotte, in hopes of boosting her aunt's energy level. Walking into the small, cozy home, Bella found Charlotte propped on the sofa with her eyes closed while a game show played on the television.

Charlotte still wore the dark shoes and black clothing from her current job as a stylist at a salon. Her hair, previously her shining glory as she changed styles and colors with each season, now covered her head with a short brown and gray fuzz.

Despite cosmetic concealer, violet smudges of weariness showed beneath her eyes. Her eyelids fluttered and she glanced up at Bella, her lips lifting in a smile. "Look at you. You brought me food again. You're trying to make me fat," she complained as she sat up and patted the sofa for Bella to join her.

"This way you don't have to fix it. You can just eat it. Would you like to eat here or in the kitchen?"

"Here is fine," Charlotte said and Bella pulled out a TV tray.

"What would you like to drink?" Bella asked.

"I can get it myself," Charlotte said and started to rise.

"I'm already up," Bella argued. "Water, soda, tea?"

"Hot tea," Charlotte said and shook her head. "You fuss over me too much."

"Not at all," Bella said as she put the tea kettle on in the adjoining kitchen. "If I'd known what you were going through, I would have come back to help you with your treatments."

"You needed that trip. You'd earned it. I can take care of myself," Charlotte insisted as Bella brought her the cup of tea.

"I would have made it easier for you," Bella said, sitting next to the woman who had raised her. "I could have helped with the business."

Charlotte sighed. "Well, I overestimated my stamina, and losing the spas has been a hard pill to swallow. But I did the best I could. You have to stop taking responsibility for things that you can't control."

"But—"

"Really," Charlotte said sharply then her face

softened. "You can't spend your life trying to be the polar opposite of your mother. You've worked hard, earned your degree in college, did rescue work overseas. Now it's time for you to enjoy your life, do what you want to do. You've got to stop worrying about me."

Bella bit her tongue, but nothing her aunt said made her feel one bit less responsible. How was it fair that Bella had lived her dream when her aunt had lost hers? It just wasn't right. If there was a way to make it up to Charlotte, she should do it.

Unable to sleep, Bella racked her brain for any possibilities. She'd already approached several banks and been turned down flat. Her only hope was Michael Medici.

The mere thought of him gave her shivers. That didn't stop her, however, from calling his assistant to make an appointment to meet him at his office. Luckily, or not, she was told Michael would meet her that afternoon. It would be tight since she was scheduled to work the evening shift at the restaurant, but she knew she needed to do this as soon as possible before she talked herself out of it.

Shoring up her courage, she strode into his office when his assistant gave her the go-ahead. He stood as she entered and with her heart pounding in her ears, she met his gaze. "I'll take the deal."

He raised his eyebrow and nodded.

"With conditions," she added.

His dark gaze turned inscrutable. "What conditions?" he asked in a velvet voice.

"That we set a time limit for our—" She floundered for the right word. "Involvement."

"Agreed. One year," he said. "After that time, you and I can determine if we want to continue."

She gave a quick nod. "And my aunt is never ever to know that I agreed to this in order for her to get her business."

"You have my word," he said.

She wanted more than his word. She wanted a document signed in blood, preferably his.

Her expression must have revealed her doubt because he gave a cynical chuckle. "You'll know you can count on my word soon enough."

"There are other things we need to work out. Is this going to be totally secret? Are we supposed to pretend that we're just acquaintances?"

"We can negotiate that later. I'll expect you to be exclusive."

"And what about you?" she asked.

He lifted his eyebrows again then allowed his gaze to fall over her. "Based on our experience in bed, I think you'll be able to take care of my appetite."

Bella felt a surprising rush of heat race through her. How did the man generate so much excitement without even touching her? She glanced at her watch and cleared her throat. "Okay, I think we've covered the basics. I need to get to work."

"You can quit the restaurant," he said without batting an eye.

"No, I can't. I need the extra money to help my aunt," she said.

"Now, now," he said. "You'll be busy helping her at the spa. Your nights belong to me."

Three days later, Michael was working late as usual when his cell phone rang. *Bella,* he saw from the caller ID and picked up. "This is a surprise."

"I got off a little early. I've worked the last few nights." She hesitated a half beat. "I gave my notice."

"Where are you?" he asked.

"In the parking lot of your office," she said breathlessly.

Michael felt an immediate surge of arousal. During every spare minute he'd thought about Bella, her body, her response, the sound of her voice, her violet eyes filled with passion. "I'll be down in a couple minutes," he said.

Wrapping up his work and turning off his laptop, he strode downstairs, a sense of eagerness running through him like white lightning. He didn't know why this woman affected him so much, but he'd decided not to question it and enjoy her. Every inch of her.

He walked outside and saw the lights from her Volkswagen flicker, guiding him to her vehicle. He opened the door and allowed himself the luxury of looking at her from head to toe. After all, for the next year, she was his.

Still dressed in her white shirt and black skirt from work, she gazed at him with trepidation, her white teeth biting the side of her upper lip. Her hands clasped the steering wheel in a white-knuckle grip.

"Hi," he said.

"Hi," she said and seemed to hold her breath. "I wasn't sure when I was supposed to start."

He couldn't quite swallow a chuckle at her tension. She glanced at him in consternation.

"Why don't we just start with dinner at my place?" he asked.

"Now?"

He nodded. "What do you want?"

She blinked and paused a long moment. "A hot fudge sundae and sparkling wine."

"That can be arranged," he said. "Would you like to ride in my car or follow—"

"Follow," she said, her grip tightening on the steering wheel. "I'll follow you."

On the way home, he called his housekeeper and ordered filet mignon for two, baked potatoes, a hot fudge sundae and a bottle of Cristal champagne. Driving through the guarded entrance to his subdivision, he glanced at his rearview mirror to make sure Bella made it through.

He pulled his Viper into his garage, got out and motioned for her to pull into the space on the other side of his SUV.

He watched her step out of her Volkswagen. Despite the wariness on her face, he remembered how she'd felt in his arms that night. She was a lot more trouble than any of his other lovers had been, but she was worth it. He took her arm and guided her up the stairs into the house.

She glanced around as if she were taking in every detail. Michael was usually so intent on a project or task that he barely noticed his surroundings.

"It's beautiful. Sophisticated, but comfortable," she said as they approached the large den with a cathedral ceiling and gas fireplace already lit. She glanced at him. "Do you have it on a timer?"

He shook his head. "My housekeeper took care of it. You act as if you've never seen my house before."

She bit her lip and gave a half smile. "I guess I was a little distracted the last time I was here."

Her grudging confession sent a sharp twist of challenge through him. She had been honey in his hands and he would seduce her to the same softness again. But she was still tense, so he would need to take it slow. "You mentioned something about a hot fudge sundae. Would you like a steak first?"

Her eyes widened and she sniffed the air. "I thought I smelled something cooking. How did you manage that so quickly?"

He shrugged. "Just like I said: A simple call to my housekeeper. Would you like to dine by the fire?"

"That would be lovely," she said.

He nodded. "Let me take your coat."

She met his gaze and slowly removed her coat, her eyes full of reservation over the loss of even one article of clothing. She glanced away and brushed her hands together as she moved toward the fire.

"I'll change clothes and be back down in a minute. Make yourself comfortable."

Two glasses of champagne, filet and baked potato later, Bella felt herself loosen up slightly. She was still tense, still wondered how their arrangement was going to work.

"So, tell me your life story," he said with a slight upturn of his mouth that was incredibly seductive.

"You know my aunt's situation," she said, taking a sip of water.

"What about your parents?"

"Never knew my father, although I'm told he and my mother were briefly married after a Vegas wedding," she said. "My mother left me with Aunt Charlotte when I was two." Rationally, she knew she was lucky she'd been given to Charlotte. Deep inside though, every once in a while, she wondered why she hadn't been enough for her mother to want to keep her and for her father to at least want to know her.

"So your aunt raised you," he said. "That's why

you're so devoted to her. You glossed over that the night we were together."

She nodded. "It requires an extended explanation. My Aunt Charlotte has always been there for me whenever I needed her. My mother wasn't cut out for mothering. She moved out to California and sent money to Charlotte every now and then. She came to visit me twice—once when I was six and the last time when I was twelve."

"Do you talk to her now?"

"She died a couple years ago."

"We have that in common," he said. "My father was killed when my brothers and I were very young."

"You told me that. I think that was part of what made me feel at ease with you. You mentioned something about one of your brothers dying with him, but you didn't say who had raised the rest of you."

"Foster care for all of us. Separate homes."

She winced. "That had to have been difficult."

"It could have been worse," he said with a shrug. "Each of us turned out successfully. In my case, I spent my teenage years in a group home and was lucky enough to have a mentor."

"Do you see your brothers now?"

"Sometimes. Not on a regular basis. We're all busy."

"Hmm. You need a tradition."

"Why is that?"

"A tradition forces you to get together. My aunt does this with my cousins and relatives at least twice a year. Once at Christmas, then during the summer for barbecue and games weekend."

"Does shooting pool count?"

"It can. Good food helps."

"Oh yeah? Junk food works for us. Buffalo wings, pizza. Maybe with both my brothers married, the women will try to civilize us."

"Maybe so," she said. "I hear marriage can do that sometimes with men."

"I guess I'll always be uncivilized, then because I don't plan to ever get married."

His flat statement comforted her in a bizarre way. After her breakup with Stephen, she couldn't imagine giving another man her heart, if she even had a heart to give. She lifted her glass and met his gaze. "That makes two of us."

Four

Michael held her gaze for a long moment then pulled her toward him. "I've been watching your mouth all night," he said and lowered his lips to hers.

An unexpected sigh eased out of her. His mouth was warm, firm yet soft and addictive. She wanted to taste him, taste all of him. He fascinated her with his confidence, power and intuitiveness.

She lifted her hands to run her fingers through his wavy hair. A half breath later, he pulled her into his lap and devoured her mouth. The chemistry between them was taut and combustible. Every time he slid his tongue over hers, she felt something inside her twist tighter.

He slid his hands to her shoulders then lower to her breasts. Her nipples stood against her shirt, taut and needy. He rubbed them with his thumbs, drawing them into tight orbs. She felt a corresponding twist in her nether regions.

"You feel so good," he muttered against her mouth. "I have to have you again."

His voice rumbled through her, making her heart pound. He slanted his mouth against hers, taking her more fully. She craved the sensation of his mouth and tongue. His need salved a hollow place deep inside her.

She felt his hands move to the center of her white shirt. A tugging sensation followed and cool air flowed over her bare chest. His lips still holding hers, he dipped his thumbs into the cups of her bra, touching her nipples.

She gasped at the sensation.

"Good?" he murmured. "Do you want more? I can give it to you."

She felt herself grow liquid beneath his caresses. Each stroke of his thumb made her more restless. He skimmed one of his hands down the side of her waist then to the front of her skirt.

"It's a damn shame you're wearing tights," he said.

A shiver raced through her at his sexy complaint.

"I think it's time for us to go to my room," he said.

Suddenly, as if the room turned upside down, it hit her that this would be the beginning of the deal. She froze. He stood and pulled her to her feet.

She stared at him, struck with the awful feeling of being at his mercy. Unable to keep herself from breathing hard, she closed her eyes and told herself it would be okay. It was just sex. Since she'd lost the man she really loved, it would only ever be…sex.

"Bella," he said, his hand cupping her chin. "Look at me."

She swallowed hard over her conflicting emotions and opened her eyes, catching his gaze for several heart-twisting beats.

He gave a sigh and a grimace then slid his hand down to capture hers. "You've had a busy day, haven't you?"

"Yes, I have."

He nodded. "You should get some rest," he said and led her out of the den.

"Where—"

"I have a room for you," he said. "Let the house-keeper know if you need anything. Her name is Trena."

"But I thought," she said, confused by the change of plans.

He stopped in front of a door and looked down at her. "I've never had to force a woman. I'm not about to start now."

She bit her upper lip with her bottom teeth. "This is new for me. I haven't done anything like this before."

"Neither have I," he said and lifted his eyebrow in a combination of amusement and irony. "Don't count on me being patient for long. No one has ever accused me of letting the grass grow under my feet. I'll send Trena in to check on you in a few minutes. Good night."

Bella put her face in her hands after he closed the door. Shocked, she shook her head and glanced around the bedroom. Furnished in sea-blues and greens, the soft tones of the room immediately took her anxiety down several notches. Flanked by windows covered with airy curtains, a large comfortable-looking bed beckoned from the opposite wall. A large painting of an ocean scene hung above the bed, making her wonder if Michael enjoyed the sea as much as she did.

The bed stand held a collection of books, a small sea-shell lamp and a tray for a late-night snack. A long cherry bureau with a small padded chair occupied another. The room had clearly been furnished with comfort in mind.

She walked into the connecting bath and almost drooled. Marble double sinks, a large Jacuzzi tub, shower that would easily accommodate two and flowering plants. Much nicer than her one-bedroom apartment.

Don't get used to it, she warned herself.

A knock sounded on the door and Bella opened it to a competent-looking woman dressed in black slacks and a white shirt. "Miss St. Clair. I'm Trena, one of Mr. Medici's staff. Welcome. Please tell me what I can do to make your stay more comfortable."

Bella glanced around. "I can't think of anything. The room is wonderful."

Trena nodded. "Good. There's water, wine, beer and soda in the mini bar along with some snacks. There's a fresh bathrobe hanging in the closet and toiletries in the bathroom."

"Thank you. Oh, I just realized I don't have pajamas," Bella said. She hadn't been sure whether she would be staying the night or not. "Perhaps a T-shirt?"

"No problem."

"Again, thank you. I'll just go get my change of clothing from my car."

"If you'll give me the keys, I can do that for you," Trena offered.

"Oh, no," she protested. "I can do that myself."

Trena looked offended. "Please allow me. Mr. Medici emphasized that he wants you to relax. It's my job and I take pride in doing a good job."

She blinked at the woman's firm tone. "Okay, thank you."

"My pleasure. I'll be back in just a moment."

Wow, Bella thought. The woman brought service to a new level. She shouldn't be surprised. Michael Medici would employ only the best and probably paid very well. Stifling a nervous chuckle, she envisioned Trena shaking her finger at her and saying, *"You must relax."*

Just moments later, Trena returned with Bella's tote bag of clothes she always kept in the back of her car in case she wanted to change before or after work at the restaurant. She also brought her a soft extra-large T-shirt. Staring at a painting of a pink shell on the wall, she wondered about Michael.

What kind of man would make a deal to bail out her aunt in exchange for an affair with her?

Who was she to cast stones? After all, what kind of woman would accept his offer?

She thought it would take forever to fall asleep so she picked up a book on the nightstand, a thriller. Seven hours later, she awakened to the smell of fresh-brewed coffee with the thriller on her chest.

Shaking her head, she quickly realized she wasn't in her own bed. Her sheets weren't this soft, her mattress not so…perfect. Scrambling out of bed, she pulled on her clothes and splashed water on her face and brushed her teeth and hair. And added lip gloss.

Calm, calm, she told herself and walked into the kitchen.

A bald, black man standing next to the coffeemaker looked up at her. "Miss St. Clair?"

She nodded. "Yes."

His mouth stretched into a wide grin of reassurance. "Pleasure to meet you. I'm Sam. Mr. Medici instructed me to fix your breakfast. Would you like a cappuccino?"

"It's nice to meet you, too, Sam. There's no need for you to fix my breakfast."

Sam's smile fell. "My instructions are to feed you a good breakfast. I wish to do as he instructed."

Geez, Michael sure had his staff trained. "I'm not really hungry…."

"But a cappuccino? Latte?"

She sighed, not entirely comfortable with others serving her to such a degree. "Latte, thank you. Where is Mr. Medici?"

Sam chuckled. "Long gone. That man rises before the sun. Very rarely does he sleep late. He left a note for you," he said and held out an envelope. "Would you like oatmeal pancakes? I make very good pancakes."

She smiled at his gentle, persuasive tone. "Sold." She opened the envelope and read the handwritten three-line note. *Bring your aunt to my office at 9:00 a.m. for a planning meeting tomorrow morning. Enjoy Sam's pancakes. Looking forward to our next night together. Michael.*

Her heart rose to her throat. He was sticking to his part. She would need to meet her end of the deal, too. Pancakes? How could she possibly?

"I have pure maple syrup, too," Sam said.

Bella took a deep breath and sighed. What the hell. "Why not."

One day later, she took her aunt to meet Michael. Still bracing herself for the possibility that Michael would back out, she just told Charlotte that they were meeting someone for a special business consultation. Although

Charlotte pounded her with questions, Bella remained vague.

"I wish you would tell me what this is about," Charlotte said, adjusting her vivid pink suit as the elevator climbed to the floor of MM, Inc.

"You'll know soon enough," Bella said, adjusting her own black jacket. The elevator dinged their arrival and Bella led the way to Michael's office.

"How do you know this man?"

"I met him through my job," Bella said.

"At a bar?" Charlotte asked.

"He's the owner," Bella explained then pushed open the door to the office. She lifted her lips into a smile for Michael's assistant. "Hi. Bella St. Clair and Charlotte Ambrose to see Mr. Medici."

His assistant nodded. "He's expecting you." She announced their arrival and waved toward his office door. "Please, go ahead in."

Charlotte cast Bella a suspicious glance. "What have you gotten me into?"

"It's good," Bella promised as they walked toward the door and she pushed it open. "But I think it would be better for Mr. Medici to talk about it."

Michael rose to meet them. "Bella," he said. "Ms. Ambrose. It's good to meet you," he said to Charlotte. "Bella has told me so much about you, but she didn't tell me what a lovely woman you are."

Charlotte accepted his handshake and slid a sideways glance at Bella. "Thank you. I wish I could say the same about her telling me about you."

Michael gave a chuckle. "I'm sure she was just trying to protect you. Let's sit down and talk about the business plan for your spa."

Charlotte stopped cold. "Excuse me? I lost my spa business to the bank."

Michael glanced at Bella and made a tsk-ing sound. "You really did keep her in the dark, didn't you?"

Charlotte frowned. "I would appreciate an explanation."

"The bank took over your business and I bought it. After discussions with Bella, I've made the decision to finance and codirect a relaunch of one Charlotte's Signature Spa."

Charlotte stared at him in amazement. "Codirect?" she echoed. "Relaunch?"

He nodded. "Yes. Let me show you the plan."

Over the next hour, Bella watched her aunt's demeanor change from doubt to hope and excitement. By the end of the meeting, Bella knew she had made the right choice in helping her. The illness and loss of her business had robbed Charlotte of her natural drive and optimism.

"I can't tell you how grateful I am for this opportunity. Your backing means—" Charlotte glanced back and forth between Michael and Bella, her eyes filling with tears. "Oh, no. I'm going to embarrass myself. Please excuse me for a moment," she said, standing. "Could you tell me where the powder room is?"

Concerned, Bella followed her aunt to her feet. "Charlotte?"

Michael also rose and Charlotte waved her hand. "No. You stay here. I just need a moment to compose myself."

"The restroom is in the outer office," Michael said and Charlotte left his office. "Is she okay?" he asked Bella.

Full of her own overwhelming emotion, Bella wrapped her arms around her waist and nodded. "She's stunned. She'd lost all hope of rebuilding her business. I probably should have at least given her a hint, but I didn't want her to be disappointed if—" She paused, meeting his intent gaze. "If things didn't work out."

"Why wouldn't they? I gave you my word, didn't I?"

"Yes, you did," she said, and felt something inside her twist and knot at his expression. He would have her again. She felt it and knew it, just as he did.

"I'll meet you at my house tonight," he said, his voice low.

Awareness and anticipation rippled through Bella. "It will be late," she said. "I have to work."

Michael frowned in impatience. The door to his office burst open and Charlotte strode inside with a smile on her face and a new sparkle in her eye. "When do we start?"

Michael laughed. "Bella told me you were a fireball. She also indicated that you already have a job, so as soon as you give notice we can move ahead."

"I don't need to wait," Charlotte argued. "I can work when my job is done for the day."

He shook his head firmly. "I don't want you to overdo."

"But—"

"It's not just bad for your health. It's bad for business," Michael said. "What we want to create is an environment of success that won't put too much stress on Bella or you. We want to move at a reasonable pace, not lightning."

"He's right," Bella said, admiring Michael's approach with both her aunt and the business. "And since I'll be working with you for at least this first year, I'll be able to tell if you're doing too much."

Charlotte shook her head. "You worry too much

about me. You're young. You should be pursuing your own career goals. I'm fine."

"I'm more than happy to do this with you," Bella said. "It will be an adventure."

"Yes," Michael said. "An excellent way of looking at it. An adventure."

By the expression in his eyes, however, Bella suspected he wasn't talking about the spa.

That night after work, Bella tamped down her feelings of apprehension and got into her car to drive to Michael's house. Using the rhythm of the windshield wipers as a cadence, she talked herself into calm confidence. Succeeding until the coughs and sputters of her ordinarily reliable Volkswagen jarred her out of it. "No, no, no," she murmured. She pressed on the gas and her car stalled.

Flustered, she tried to start it again and the engine coughed to life. Relief washed over her and she made it several more yards before the car shuddered again, refusing to restart. Something was clearly wrong. It revved to feeble life briefly and she managed to pull it on to the side of the road.

She got out of the car to stare at a bunch of hoses, boxes and wires under the hood. It could have been run by squirrels for all she knew. The cold rain poured over her head, drenching her jacket.

Sighing, she got back in the car and reviewed her options. She'd neglected to renew her car service since she'd returned from overseas, so her customer number was now defunct. She refused to call her aunt and bother her at this late hour. Reluctantly, she accepted her last choice and tried to dial Michael's cell number.

Her cell phone, however, gave her the impudent message. No service.

Damn. Maybe someone was trying to tell her something. That she'd best try to find a way out of her arrangement with Michael.

Bella leaned her head against the side window of her car, recalling the joy on her aunt's face when she'd learned she would get a second chance with her business. That was worth everything. A deal was a deal.

The rain appeared to have slowed down, and if she remembered correctly, Michael's gated subdivision was only about a mile from here. Walking alone at night wasn't the best choice for a woman, but she didn't want to stay in her car all night either. Either choice meant danger.

Five

Michael narrowed his eyes as he glanced at his watch. Bella wasn't going to show. He should have known that her wide eyes hid deceit. She'd tricked him into believing she would accept his deal and now she wanted out. Two nights ago, he'd been certain she'd just been nervous. Now, he wasn't sure. A bitter taste filled his mouth. What she didn't understand was that he could still pull the plug on her aunt's spa.

His cell phone rang, distracting him. The number on the caller ID was unfamiliar. "Hello," he said.

"Mr. Medici?" a man said.

"Yes, this is Michael Medici."

"This is Frank Borne, security for the neighborhood. I hate to bother you, but there's a woman here who says she knows you and she needs a ride to your house."

"What?" Michael asked.

He gave a half chuckle. "Poor thing is drenched. I'd drive her to your house myself, but I'm not supposed to leave the gatehouse."

"I'll be right there," he said, wondering what in hell had happened. Although he could have sent one of his staff to collect *the woman* whom he was sure was Bella, he preferred to handle this task himself. He turned on his windshield wipers to fight off the downpour as he drove the short distance to the gatehouse.

As soon as he pulled next to the small building, Bella dashed out. He flipped the locks and she plopped into the passenger seat. Her dark hair was plastered to her scalp, her huge violet eyes a stark contrast against her pale skin, her plum-colored lips pursed into a frown.

"What—"

She lifted her hand and shook her head. "You have no idea what I've been through to get here tonight. If I believed in heebie-jeebie kind of stuff, I would think someone was trying to tell me not to come to your house. My car stalled out on me just after I got off the interstate. My car service is defunct because I forgot to renew it. But it wouldn't have helped anyway because my cell phone said *No Service* every time I tried to make a call. It wasn't raining that much when I first started walking—"

Appalled that she'd been wandering around alone after dark, he cut her off. "Tell me you weren't walking on Travers Road after eleven o'clock at night."

"Well, what else could I do? Flag someone down? That didn't seem like a smart idea."

Michael drove them back, grinding his teeth as she continued.

"I did take my umbrella, but it was useless against this wind. I misjudged the distance a bit."

He pulled to a stop in the garage. "This won't be happening again," he said, surprised at the intensity of his protectiveness for her. He hadn't known her long enough to feel this way.

"Lord, I hope not," she said, rolling her eyes.

The way his gut clenched irritated the hell out of him. He swore. There was only one solution. "I'm getting you a new cell phone and service and new car," he said and got out of the car.

He opened her car door to find her gaping at him. "New car," she echoed. "You're crazy. I love my VW. It's never given me any trouble," she said then corrected herself. "Until tonight."

"Stranding you at night on Travers Road is enough of a reason to replace your car. Do you realize what could have happened to you?" She looked like a drowned little girl. Resisting the urge to pick her up and carry her, he extended his hand to her and led her into the house. "I'll send one of my staff to take care of your car. Do you need anything out of it?"

"I left an overnight bag in the backseat, but about a new car, I can't let you—"

He lifted his hand to cut her off as he pulled his BlackBerry out of his pocket and punched a number. "Jay, I need you to arrange for a tow—a VW on Travers. I'll leave the key on the table in the foyer." He extended his palm for Bella to give him the key. "There should be an overnight bag inside. Just drop it in the foyer. Thanks," he said and turned to her. "Now, I want you to take a hot shower." He glanced at the time on his BlackBerry. "You've got two minutes."

"To shower?" she said, her eyes round with surprise.

"Until I join you," he countered.

He hadn't thought it possible, but her eyes widened even more. "Oh," she managed, her lips forming a tempting circle of invitation. She stood as if her feet were superglued to the floor.

"Bella," he said gently.

"Yes?"

"You're down to one minute forty-five seconds."

She turned and flew down the hall.

Prying off the wet garments that clung to her as she entered the bedroom, Bella snapped her chattering teeth together. She raced to the bathroom to turn on the jets to the shower and wondered what Michael would have done if she'd said she didn't want a shower. It would have been a lie, of course. This wasn't how she'd pictured the consummation of their bargain.

Telling herself to stop thinking, she jumped into the shower and closed her eyes, treasuring the few seconds she would enjoy alone under the spray.

Sure enough, the shower door opened behind her and she felt a shot of cool air before she heard Michael's feet step on to the wet tile. He would be totally naked. The memory of his strong, male body made her pulse race.

"Is the water warm enough?"

She nodded, focusing on the tile wall in front of her.

"Want me to wash your back?"

She opened her mouth to say she could do it herself, but his hands on her bare skin stopped her. He massaged her shoulders and neck, making her relax despite herself. He skimmed his hands down the outside of her arms then back up along the inside. The sensation was both soothing and erotic. The warm water washed away her resistance.

"Not so bad, is it?" he asked.

"No, it's…" She took a deep breath.

He continued to touch her, sliding his hands over the sides of her waist and down over her hips. A slow drag of want pulled through her, starting below her skin and fanning out. Although he hadn't touched them, her breasts grew heavy and her nipples tightened.

Surprise slid through her. How was it so easy for him to turn her nerves into arousal? Must've been the shower, she thought. Not the man. But then he guided her around to face him, pushed her wet hair from her face and brushed his lips over her cheeks. With the water streaming down on them, he took her mouth and her pulse spiked again. Her eyelids fluttering against the shower drops, she caught flashes of his body, his broad shoulders and slick, tanned skin. Another flash, his flat abdomen and hard erection.

She moved closer to him and heard his breath hitch when her naked body slid against his. "I've wanted you since that night we spent together." He slid his tongue past her lips and a primitive yearning beat like a drum inside her.

There were all kinds of reasons she shouldn't want him. This was just supposed to be sex, but for some reason, it felt like more. She felt protected and desired at the same time. She couldn't remember feeling this sensual even with…

Michael lifted his hands to her breasts, short-circuiting her brain. Half a breath later, he lowered his head and took her wet nipples into his mouth. The sight and sensation was so erotic she couldn't look away. He slid lower still and kissed her intimately. Her knees turned to liquid.

"Wrap your legs around me," he said in a low voice. Catching her against him, he picked her up, turned off the water and carried her out of the shower. He grabbed a couple of plush towels folded on a small bathroom table and pulled one around her as he strode into the darkened bedroom.

He put her on the bed and followed her down, his eyes plundering her the way she suspected he planned to plunder her body. A shiver of anticipation raced through her.

"Cold?" he asked.

She nodded, reaching up to stroke a drop of water from his forehead. He captured her hand and lifted it to his mouth. "I can get you warm," he promised and slid his hand down between her legs where he found her swollen.

His fingers sent her in a sudden spiral upward. Unable to contain her response, she arched upward.

He growled at her response and pushed her thighs apart. In one thrust, he filled her to the brim.

Bella gasped, feeling her body shake and tremble around him. She clung to him as he stroked her in her most secret place. Her breath meshed with his and her climax ripped through her like a lightning bolt. A second later, she felt Michael stiffen, groaning in release.

A full moment passed and Bella began to understand why she'd been so hesitant about becoming Michael's lover. He had just taken full possession of her mind and body, and that made him a very dangerous man.

After a full night of lovemaking, Michael awakened refreshed. Still out like a light, Bella sprawled stomach down on his bed. Smiling to himself, he wouldn't bother her this morning. She'd had a rough night in more ways than one.

He left the bed and went to his in-house gym down the hall. He did the elliptical and followed up with weights. Working out was just one more way of staying strong and focused for Michael. Like his brothers, he never wanted to be at the mercy of any person or circumstance. He returned to his suite to take a shower. Bella still slept soundly. After dressing, he went downstairs and read *The Wall Street Journal* as he ate the breakfast his staff prepared for him.

Just as he stood to leave, Bella stumbled into the kitchen, dressed in a bathrobe too large for her and pushed her mussed hair from her face. She tugged at the lapels of the robe and stared at him. "It's not even six o'clock," she said. "How long have you been up?"

"Since just before five," he said with a shrug. "How are you?"

"Four something," she said, aghast. "After the night we—" She paused and lowered her voice. "We had you get up at four in the morning?"

"Well, I didn't walk a mile in the rain," he pointed out, amused by the consternation on her face. "But I don't require a lot of sleep," he said and walked toward her, giving into the urge to slide his fingers over her hair. Soft hair, soft body, mysterious eyes that tugged at something deep inside him.

She met his gaze and pressed her lips together. "Oh, well, heaven help me then. I have to tell you that I'm not accustomed to the degree and amount and—" She shook her head.

"Don't worry. You'll get used to it," he joked. He

glanced at his watch. "I need to go. Make yourself at home. The staff will be happy to prepare anything you want to eat. Here is the key to a new Lexus. I think you'll find it reliable," he said and lifted her hand to press the key into her palm.

"I told you I don't want a new car," she said.

Her resistance amused him. Most women he'd dated would have been thrilled to receive a new car. In fact, a few had hinted that a luxury vehicle would be the perfect gift for any occasion. The only thing better, of course, would have been an engagement ring, and that would never have happened. "I've leased it for you. Since yours is in the shop, you need something to drive. Oh, and I'd like for you to move in."

He turned and walked toward the door.

"I don't think that's a good idea," she said as his hand touched the doorknob.

Surprised by her response, he turned around. "Why not?"

"Because then people might find out that we're involved. I don't want to have to explain our arrangement."

He felt a crackle of impatience. "I make it a policy to never explain myself."

"Yeah, well, I'm not you. Aunt Charlotte will expect an explanation from me. I never know when she'll start with her mother hen routine, even now."

Irritation nicked at him. "We'll see," he said, turning around to look at her. "In the meantime, bring some of your clothes and belongings here for convenience sake."

"Do you order everyone around like this?" she asked, crossing her arms over her chest.

"I'm decisive. I see a logical course of action and take it," he said.

"Part of your charm?" she said, a gently mocking smile playing on her lips. "What's logical about your arrangement with me?"

"I want you, and you might not want to admit it, but you want me, too. I just figured out a way to make it happen," he said, still uncomfortable with the intensity of his desire for her and the way she affected him. He had broken some of his rules to get her out of his system. He knew his response to her wouldn't last. Nothing was forever.

Since Bella was scheduled off from the restaurant, she went to her aunt's house to begin getting ready for the grand reopening. Michael had mapped out an action plan with a target date just weeks away. Inventory needed to be ordered immediately and Charlotte would want to hire staff. Bella also needed to organize customer records so they could send out a mailing. Michael had suggested several customer incentives.

His ability to detach himself emotionally bothered her. Sure, he possessed enormous insight and experience and knew how to make things happen, but she wondered how someone who seemed so cold one moment could be so hot the next.

Her skin grew warm at the memory of how passionate he'd been, how passionate she'd been. She knew his difficult childhood had made him determined not to be vulnerable, but Bella didn't believe such a thing was possible.

Pushing aside her thoughts, she dug into her tasks. Hours later, she heard the sound of the side door opening. Charlotte looked at Bella in surprise. "It's you. I wondered whose car that was. A Lexus? Did you win the lottery?"

Bella's cheeks heated. One more reason she should have refused the use of the car. "Lucky break," she said. "My Volkswagen broke down last night. The car I'm using is a rental."

"Lucky break, indeed," Charlotte said. "Enjoy it while you can. What are you working on?"

"I was going to do an inventory order list, but I thought I should check with you first," Bella said.

"Good thinking," Charlotte said. "I made one last night."

Concern rushed through her. She searched Charlotte's face for signs of weariness, but all she saw was a glow of anticipation. "You're still working your other job. I'm afraid you're doing too much."

Charlotte smiled. "I'm too excited to sit still. I thought I'd lost my chance. I can't wait to get everything ready to go."

Bella laughed and shook her head. "Force yourself to sit still every now and then, starting now." She led her aunt to a chair and urged her to take a seat. "Let me get you some water."

"But I don't need—"

"Yes you do," Bella insisted. "Don't try to do everything at once. I'm here to help you. Remember? Speaking of which, I've been working on a customer mailing list."

"Perfect," she said. "And I called a few of my former employees to ask if they could give me some quality employee recommendations and two of them said they wanted to come back to work for me."

"Wow, you're moving right along," Bella said, pleased with her aunt's sunny outlook.

"I am," Charlotte said. "Plus, I have an idea for providing a few men's services. We can give them *Sport* manicures and pedicures and carry sports magazines and *The Wall Street Journal*."

"That's a great idea."

"And who knows? Maybe you'll end up going out with one of the men who come into the Spa," Charlotte said, throwing Bella a meaningful glance.

Bella immediately shook her head. "Oh, no. I'm not interested in dating right now." Or maybe ever.

"Bella, I know you were terribly hurt when you and Stephen broke up, but you can't stop living."

"I'm still living," Bella said. "I'm just not interested in going down that road. I know I'll never feel the way I did for Stephen about another man."

"You're too young to say that," Charlotte chided.

"You always said I had an old soul," Bella returned.

Charlotte pursed her lips. "I can see I'm going to need to open your eyes to all the other fish in the sea out there."

Bella shook her head again, cringing at the note of determination in her aunt's voice. Bella absolutely didn't want her romantic status on her aunt's radar at all. "Your mission is to stay healthy, be happy and get the spa off the ground."

"We'll see," Charlotte said.

Bella frowned. That was the second time today she'd heard those words.

That night, Bella joined Michael for dinner in the den again. "I really need to get my VW back," she said, pushing the gourmet meal around her plate. She felt nervous around Michael. Hyperaware of his strength and mental prowess, she found being the subject of his undivided attention disturbing.

"Why? The Lexus is much more dependable."

"When my aunt saw it, she asked me if I'd won the lottery."

Irritation crossed his face. "Can't you just tell her you decided to lease it?"

"Not on a waitress's salary," she said.

"I could give her one, too and tell her it's part of her compensation package," he mused.

So they would be even more in his debt? Bella choked. "I don't think that's necessary. I'll be happy to get my VW back."

"I'll get it back for you with the understanding that if it becomes unreliable again, it will be replaced. And if it breaks down, you're to call the emergency number I gave you."

"Okay," she said, because she would make sure the VW didn't break down again. "Now if I can just keep her focused on the spa and not matchmaking for me, then maybe—"

"Matchmaking," he echoed. "Why?"

"When my aunt isn't sick, she's a force to be reckoned with. If she decides I should be dating, then she'll do everything possible to make sure I am."

"Interfering family members. I've never had that. My brothers and I hassle each other every now and then, but we wouldn't interfere." He took a drink from his beer. "Go ahead and tell her you're involved with me."

"Absolutely not. She would freak out if she knew this deal was dependent on you and me…" She cleared her throat. "Besides, you agreed that we would keep it—"

Michael's cell phone rang, interrupting her tirade. He glanced at the caller ID and his expression turned odd. "I need to take this," he said and rose. "Dan, you have some information about Leo?"

She watched as he strode a few steps away with his broad back facing her. Something in his demeanor tripped off her antennae. His stance was tense as if he were braced.

"Damn. Nothing," he said, his voice full of disappointment. "Anything else you can do?"

The taut silence that followed swelled with raw tension. She'd never glimpsed this kind of emotion in Michael.

"Do it, and keep me posted," Michael said then turned around.

She glimpsed a flash of powerful emotion in his eyes, but it was gone before she could identify it. He narrowed his gaze and his nostrils flared as he returned to the table.

Bella vacillated over whether to keep silent, but her curiosity and a strange concern won out. "Who's Leo?"

He met her gaze with eyes that lit like flames of the devil himself. "My brother. He was with my father when he died."

Bella winced at the visual that raced through her head. "I haven't heard you say much about him. Where is he?"

"He could be dead, but we don't know for certain." He took a long draw from his beer. "His body was never found."

"How terrible," she said and gingerly put her hand on his arm. He glanced down at her hand for a long moment, making her wonder if she should pull it away. "Are you trying to find him?"

He sighed and lifted his gaze to hers. "Always. I was the one who was supposed to be travelling with my father that day. Leo was there in my place."

Her heart wrenched at the deep-seated guilt on his face. "Oh, no. You don't really blame yourself. You were just a child. You couldn't have possibly—"

He jerked his arm away. "Enough. This subject is off limits. I'm going to bed." He stood and stalked out of the room, leaving her reeling in his wake.

The depth of the grief and guilt she'd glimpsed in his eyes shook her. Michael might project himself as a self-contained man with little emotion, but she'd just seen something different. He had clearly suffered over the loss of his brother for years. Bella wondered what that must be like, to blame oneself for the loss of a brother. Absolution would be impossible for a man like Michael. She sensed that he would be harder on himself than anyone else. In this case, he didn't have resolution either.

A yawning pain stretched inside Bella. She bit her lip, glancing into the gas fire. She felt a strange instinct to comfort him, to salve the wounds of his losses. He spoke about his upbringing in a matter-of-fact way, as if the losses had been efficiently compartmentalized. But they hadn't.

"Miss St. Clair, I'm Glenda. Can I get anything for you?" a woman said from just a few feet away.

Bella looked at Glenda, still hung up on what she'd just learned about Michael. He was human after all.

"Would you like something else to eat?" Glenda asked. "Dessert?"

Unable to imagine eating another bite, Bella shook her head. "No, but thank you very much. I'll just take my dishes to the kitchen."

"Oh, no," Glenda said. "I'll do that. Are you sure there's nothing else I can do for you?"

Bella picked up her glass of wine and took a sip for fortitude. "Nothing, thank you."

Rising, she glanced in the direction of the hallway that would take her to her room and the stairway that would take her to Michael's.

Six

He heard the door to his bedroom open and the soft pad of her feet against the hardwood floor before she stepped on to the sheepskin rugs surrounding his big bed. He heard a rustle and a softly whispered oath. She must have stumbled a little.

He couldn't suppress a twist of amusement. An illicit thrill rushed through him.

Bella was coming to him.

He heard her soft intake of breath, as if she were bracing herself. Before she'd opened the door, he'd been a turbulent mass of emotion. Now, he was… curious.

She crawled on to his bed slowly. He waited, feeling a spurt of impatience. What was she going to do? When was she—

He felt her body against his. Her bare breasts brushed

his arm. Her thighs slid against his. He felt a blast of need.

She skimmed one of her hands over his shoulder and down his chest. He felt her lips against his throat and his gut clenched at the softness, the tenderness…

Rock hard with arousal, he was more comfortable with sex and passion than tenderness. "Why are you here?" he asked, clenching his hands together, biding his time.

"I—" She made a hmm sound that vibrated against his skin. "I didn't want you to be alone."

He gave a rough chuckle. "I've been alone most of my life."

"Not tonight," she said.

In a swift but smooth motion, he pulled her on top of him. He felt her breathless gasp of surprise and even in the dark, could see her wide eyes. "If this is pity sex, you may get more than you bargained for."

She paused barely a half beat. "Pity a superhero?"

He couldn't withhold another shot of amusement, but the urgency to take her again taunted him. He took her mouth in a long kiss that made her writhe against him. He began to sweat.

"Hold on," he muttered and slid his hands down the silky skin of her back and positioned her so that his aching erection was just at the entrance of her warm femininity.

She moaned and he pushed inside a little further. It took all his control, but he wanted to feel her need, her desperation. She arched against him then lowered her mouth to his; this time, she was the pursuer. Every part of her body seemed to talk to him—her skin, her hands, her hair…

Pulling away from him, she lifted backward and kept her gaze fastened on his. He forced himself to keep his eyes open as she bit her lip and slid down, taking all of him inside her.

His ability to wait shredded, he grabbed her hips and their lovemaking turned—as it had from the beginning—into a storm of passion that sated him at the same time it made him hungry for more.

After that night, the unspoken connection between her and Michael grew stronger. When she was apart from Michael, she sometimes wondered if she imagined the tie, but when she was with him, there was no doubt. It still wasn't love, she told herself. It was passion and power, but it wasn't the sweet, comforting love she'd known with Stephen.

Progress on the spa took place swiftly. It was all Bella could do to keep her aunt from working twenty-four hours a day. Getting a second chance with the spa seemed to have given Aunt Charlotte twice as much energy. Unfortunately, Charlotte wasn't budging from her so-called mission to get Bella back in action.

So far, she'd arranged for four men to stop by to meet Bella. Two of them had asked her out, but she'd demurred.

This morning, she put away inventory that had arrived in the mail and double-checked the postcards advertising the opening. Charlotte bustled around, tinkering with the decor to accommodate the new sports grooming package for men.

A knock sounded on the glass door and Bella glanced up to spot a nice-looking man in his upper twenties. A familiar dread tugged at her. *Not again.*

Charlotte rushed to the door and gave a little squeal.

"Gabriel, it's so good to see you. Come on in. Bella, please fix Gabriel some coffee. His mother is one of my longtime clients."

"It's good to see you," Gabriel said to Charlotte while Bella dutifully poured and served his coffee. "My mother insisted that I stop by."

"Cream or sugar?" Bella asked.

He shook his head. "No, thanks. Black is fine. Is Bella your daughter?"

"In every way that counts," Charlotte said. "Gabriel is a lawyer, Bella. Isn't that impressive? I bet he might want to use some of our new services for men."

"What services?" he asked, his expression wary.

"Sports manicure and pedicure. Massage," Charlotte said. "You look like you work out."

Bella tried not to roll her eyes at her aunt's obvious flattery.

"Some," he said. "I like to run."

Charlotte nodded then frowned. "Bella, I just realized you never took lunch. Maybe you and Gabriel could—"

The door swung open and Michael walked in. Bella felt her gut twist at the sight of him. This could get interesting, she thought.

"Michael, what a nice surprise," Charlotte said. "Michael is our new business partner. If it weren't for him, the spa wouldn't exist. Michael Medici, this is Gabriel Long. He's a lawyer—his office is down the street."

Michael nodded and shook Gabriel's hand. "Gabriel," he said.

"Michael Medici. I've heard your name mentioned often by my business clients."

"I was just saying that maybe Bella and Gabriel could go grab a bite," Charlotte interjected.

Michael paused a second and shot Bella a glance that seemed to say *we did it your way, now we're doing it my way.*

"I hate to interrupt, but I had planned to ask Bella to join *me* for dinner tonight," Michael said in a charming voice that almost concealed the steel underneath.

Charlotte dropped her jaw and stared at Michael then at Bella. "Oh, I didn't know you two were—"

"We're not," Bella quickly said, inwardly wincing at the lie. She glared at Michael. "I'm just as surprised as you are by the invitation."

Cool as ever, he dipped his head. "If you're hungry, then…"

An awkward silence followed where Bella refused to give up her mutinous stance.

"Of course she is," Charlotte rushed to say, then glanced at Gabriel as if she didn't know what to do with him. "I will give you a special coupon for our sports treatments," she added as she walked him to the door. "Now, you be sure and tell your mother I said hello…"

"You agreed," Bella whispered tersely to Michael.

"It was necessary. This is becoming ridiculous. Things will be easier now. Trust me," he said in a low voice.

"You don't under—" She cut herself off as Charlotte returned.

"Michael, I'm so glad to see you," Charlotte said. "I wanted to show you some of my ideas. Bella, would you help me get some things from the inventory closet?"

Upset by the latest turn of events, Bella nodded and followed her aunt to the walk-in supply closet. Charlotte immediately turned to her. "What's your problem? Michael Medici is gorgeous."

"He's not my type," Bella said.

"Gorgeous and wealthy isn't your type, plus, he's been wonderful to us. It won't hurt you to be nice to him in return," Charlotte said firmly.

"It won't?" Bella asked. Charlotte met her eyes and instantly knew what Bella was talking about.

"This is not the same situation as your mother. Get that thought out of your mind. Michael isn't married to a woman."

Bella closed her eyes, struggling with guilt and shame. "He's not Stephen."

"No, he's not," Charlotte said. "Michael Medici is a stronger man than Stephen ever was. I never was quite sure Stephen was the best match for you, anyway."

"Charlotte," Bella said in shock. "You always liked him."

"I like dogs, too. Doesn't mean I want you to marry one. Now go on out with Michael and enjoy yourself. It hurts me knowing that you aren't having any fun in your life right now. Life is short. You need to live it while you can."

Charlotte pulled out some magazines and product catalogs and put them into Bella's hands. "Here, take these."

"What are you going to tell Michael about them?"

"I'll figure out something," Charlotte said.

An hour later, Bella sat silently in Michael's Viper as he drove the luxury car. Drumming her fingers on her denim-clad thigh, she looked out the window, still upset.

"Would you like seafood?" he asked.

"It doesn't matter, but I'm not dressed for a four-star restaurant *since this was a surprise invite.*"

Michael pulled up to the valet desk at one of the more exclusive, popular restaurants he owned in the Atlanta area. "It doesn't matter how you're dressed. You're with me and this is my restaurant," he said and got out of the car.

He escorted her inside the restaurant where the host immediately greeted him. "It's good to see you, Mr. Medici. We have a corner alcove for you."

"That will be fine," he said, touching Bella's arm as they walked to the table. She was so prickly he half expected her to swat him off.

Baffled by her reaction, he shook his head. Many women he'd dated had done everything but taken out a billboard ad announcing their involvement.

"For goodness sake, why are you so cranky? You'd think I murdered one of your relatives," he said after they sat down.

"I told you that I didn't want my aunt to know about our arrangement. You agreed."

"She doesn't know about any arrangement. All she knows is that I wanted you to join me for dinner."

"We were *supposed* to keep this secret."

"That was before she started interfering in order to get you dating. Why did she get so worked up anyway?"

"She knew about my breakup. She knew the guy I was involved with and how much I—" She broke off and shook her head. "It doesn't matter. I just didn't want her to know. And *you agreed.*"

A server appeared, eager to please. He explained the evening specials. Michael ordered a whiskey double for himself and a Hurricane for Bella.

"Hurricane?" she said after the waiter left.

"It seemed to fit with your frame of mind."

Her lips twitched, albeit reluctantly.

"So tell me why you changed your mind about letting your aunt know I want to ask you out for dinner. And I want to know more about this man who you dumped after you got back from your year in Europe."

"First, I didn't dump him. He broke it off with me before I arrived home."

"Really?" he said. "What an idiot."

Her lips twitched again as the server returned with their drinks. "Very flattering. Thank you."

"Lobster or steak?" Michael asked. "Or both?"

"I'm not that hungry."

"Both for the lady," he said, deciding for her. "Make the filet medium. I'll take the same, but make my steak rare."

"Of course, sir," the waiter said.

"I want to know more about this imbecile who dropped you," he said. "I'll bet he's kicking himself up and down the street for his stupidity now."

She gave a reluctant chuckle and shook her head, sighing. "He's engaged to a beautiful blonde."

"Oh," he said and took a sip of his whiskey. "Lucky for me."

"You are the very devil himself," she said, shaking her head again and taking a sip of her potent drink. "End of discussion about my ex."

Not likely, he thought, but shelved the subject for the moment. "Fine. Why are you overreacting about your aunt knowing we're seeing each other?"

"Because we're *not* seeing each other. We have an agreement," she said bitterly and looked away.

He narrowed his eyes, sensing there was more to the story. "What else is going on? There's more. I can see it on your face. This isn't just about you and me."

She frowned, but still didn't meet his gaze. "I didn't tell you everything about my mother. She was living in California when she died, but she wasn't married. She was the mistress of a wealthy, powerful man. A married man. I vowed never to get into that situation."

Michael paused a long moment, searching his mind for the best approach. "So that's why you're uncomfortable about your arrangement with me. This is different."

Her head snapped up. "What do you mean? I may as well be your mistress. I've made an agreement in exchange for your assistance and support."

"For one thing, I'm not married. Never will be for that matter. Secondly, you made that choice for the sake of someone very important to you. I don't get the impression your mother did the same. Besides, I wouldn't have even made the offer if I didn't believe there was a chance of making the business a success."

She stared at him in surprise. "Really?"

"Really," he said. "I broke a few rules of my own for you, but not all of them. So we're on more equal ground than you imagined. You can enjoy your lobster and steak without remorse."

She looked at him, her mesmerizing eyes glowing at him, doing strange things to his insides. "Interesting," she said. "If we're on equal ground, then I'd like to ask you some questions."

Michael's gut clenched. "Such as?"

"Favorite dessert?"

He blinked then chuckled at her curiously. "Tiramisu."

"Your Italian roots are showing."

"I could prepare a lasagna for you that would make you forget every other pasta you've ever eaten."

"True?" she asked.

"True," he said.

"Okay, you're on. I want that lasagna. When is your birthday?"

"Next month, but I don't celebrate it," he said.

"Why not?"

"It's just another day. Why do you ask?"

"Because I want to know more about you. How did you celebrate your birthday when you were young?" she asked. "Before your father died."

"With a favorite meal, small gifts and dessert. That was a long time ago."

"You haven't celebrated it since you reconnected with your brothers?" she asked, a sliver of outrage in her voice.

He shook his head. "We're all too busy. Sometimes they remember to call. That's more than I got when I was in the foster home."

She frowned in disapproval. "Have all of you looked for Leo?"

His sense of humor at her questions faded. "One way or another."

"What do you remember about him?" she asked.

Michael paused, resisting the memories for a moment because he never remembered without subsequent pain and heavy, heavy guilt. "He was a fighter," Michael said. "He was only a year older than I was, and I did my best to keep up with all of them, but Leo was tough. Hell, he would even try to take on Damien. That never lasted long. Damien would just pin him down until he agreed to quit. Then Leo would get up and take another quick swipe before he ran off."

"Sounds like he was a pistol," Bella said with a soft smile.

He nodded. "Yeah, we all were, but he seemed to run full tilt from the minute he woke up until the minute he went to sleep. He was always afraid of missing something…." His chest squeezed tight, making the words difficult. He cleared his throat. "He liked animals. He was always bringing home a stray something and Dad would have to find another home for it because my mother said she had too many two-legged animals to take care of."

"And they never found any sign of him?" she said, more than asked, shaking her head.

"Every body was recovered except his," he said and the old determination rolled through him again. "If it's the last thing I do, I'm going to find him."

Bella leaned forward and slid her hand across the table to touch his. "I believe you will."

Something inside him eased at her confidence in him. He knew it wasn't based on flattery because she'd essentially already gotten what she wanted from him and she was still pissed that he'd pushed her into their affair. Soon enough she'd realize that he'd done what needed to be done for both of them.

He captured her hand with his. "Your turn for questions is over. My turn now. What's your favorite dessert?"

"Double-chocolate brownies with frosting," she said with a guilty expression on her face. "Decadent."

"Just like you," he said.

Her eyes lit with arousal but she looked away as if

she was determined to fight her attraction to him. That irritated the hell out of him. There would be no denial from any part of her when he took her tonight in his bed.

Seven

On Saturday morning, Michael surprised himself by sleeping an entire hour later than usual. He did his usual workout and was surprised even more at the sight of Bella dressed in jeans, T-shirt, and tennis shoes and her head covered by a bandana, walking out of the room where she kept her belongings.

"You're up early," he said.

"I'm painting today," she said.

He frowned. "It didn't look like the spa needed it."

"I'm not painting the spa. I'm volunteering—painting a children's activity center downtown."

"That's nice of you," he said.

"They need help with some repairs if you're interested. If you're handy, I hear they need some help with wiring and the gas heater."

"You sound like Damien," he said, thinking of his

oldest brother. "He started building houses for charity and keeps telling Rafe and me that we should do the same."

"Why don't you?"

"I donate generously to several charities. My money is more valuable than my manpower."

"Do you mentor anyone?"

Her question took him off guard. "No. My schedule is packed. It wouldn't be fair to promise to mentor someone with the limited time I have."

"Hmm," she said.

Her noncommittal sound irritated him and he narrowed his eyes. Most would have heeded his expression as a warning.

"It's a good thing your mentor made the time he did for you, isn't it?"

No one besides his brothers would dare get in his face like she did. "My mentor was retired. I'm not."

"Excuses, excuses," she said, a smile playing around her lips. "But I understand if you're afraid of getting involved."

"*Afraid,*" he echoed, snatching her hand and pulling her against him. "You aren't trying to manipulate me into charity involvement, are you?"

She paused a half beat. "Yes. Is it working?"

He couldn't help chuckling. "Not at all."

"Okay, no goading," she said. "I dare you to come down to the community children's center and help." She met his gaze, her lips lifted in a sultry half smile. She tossed her head and lifted her chin. "See ya if you're brave enough." She turned and walked away, her saucy butt swinging from side to side as she exited his house.

"Witch," he muttered and dismissed her so-called dare. He had real work to do. Walking to his office, he sat down with his laptop and crunched numbers. He worked without pausing for the next hour and a half.

The second he stopped, silence closed around him like a thick cloud. Bella and her dare jabbed at him. Silly, he thought. Stupid. A waste of time. Bella was a misplaced do-gooder. Children didn't need paint. They needed...parents.

The twinge inside him took him by surprise. He frowned at the odd sensation and shrugged, turning back to his number crunching, but his concentration came and went.

Ten minutes later, he sighed, swearing under his breath and leaned back in his leather chair. Raking his hand through his hair, he shook his head. Stupid dare, he thought, remembering the expression in her mesmerizing, nearly purple eyes.

In the long run, how much did a fresh coat of paint really matter? Two more minutes of denial rolled through his brain and he tossed his pen at his desk and turned off his laptop. What a surprise. He toyed with the idea of joining her. He liked the notion of surprising her. He liked the idea of doing something with his hands other than using his laptop or BlackBerry. Even the devil had a conscience. Or perhaps the devil couldn't resist a dare from a woman with black hair and purple eyes.

Bella continued edging the walls of one of the playrooms. She much preferred rolling paint on the walls because that part of the job was easier and more rewarding, but edging was crucial to the finished product. She would take her turn with the roller later on.

"Sandwich? Water?" Rose, a mother of one of the

children who visited the center, offered as she carried a tray.

Bella smiled and lifted her water bottle, having chatted with the young woman earlier that morning. "I'm still good, thank you. How's it going in the other rooms?" she asked as she turned back to edging.

"Very well, except the service man hasn't arrived to fix the heater," Rose said. "It's gas and I'm really concerned about the safety if—" She broke off. "Oh, hello," she said, her voice a bit breathless. "Can I help you?"

"I wondered if you could use two more hands," Michael said.

Surprised, Bella whipped around and kicked over her paint can. "Oh, no." She bent down to right it, but he caught it first. Her face mere inches from his, she felt her heart race.

He gave a half grin that made her stomach dip. "I didn't know you were planning on painting the floor."

She scowled. "It's your fault. You surprised me. I was sure you weren't coming. What made you?" Realization hit her and she answered for him. "The dare."

"I don't accept every dare. It depends on the source and actual dare."

"Well, I feel honored," she said and picked up an extra brush and put it in his hand. "Rose, this is Michael Medici. Rose's son takes part in the center's activities," Bella said.

"Good to meet you," he said.

Rose's eyes were wide with admiration. "Good to meet you, Mr. Medici. I'm so grateful for your help. Excuse me while I check on my son."

"I'm thrilled for you to finish the edging," Bella said, wondering how he would respond to the not-so-desirable task.

He glanced around the room and shrugged. "Should be cake."

Surprised again, she watched him begin and noticed he worked with speed and ease. "When did you get your painting experience?"

"Painted the entire group home twice. Once while I lived there as a teenager and once after I left. Nobody else wanted to edge, so I took that job."

"And became an expert," she said, envying his skill. "You can do it freehand."

"Part of my philosophy. If you're going to do something, be the best at it."

She should have expected that. His competitiveness was born not only from the need to survive, but from his determination to thrive. She still wondered though, why had he accepted her dare? Was there a secret tenderness underneath his hard, cynical exterior? Or was she just dreaming? She felt a hot rush of embarrassment. *Why* was she dreaming?

"Do you want anything to eat or—" A loud explosion rocked the building. "What was that?" She ran toward the door.

Michael snagged her hand. "Whoa, there," he said. "You need to get out of here and dial 911."

"I can't leave. What about the rest of the volunteers?"

"I'll work on that," he said and glanced down the hallway. "Smoke's coming from the back of the building. We don't have time to waste. Get out."

"But—"

He turned and looked her straight in the eye. "Do I need to carry you out? Because I will."

"No, but—"

"*No buts,*" he said. "Get out and make the call."

Frustrated and afraid, Bella saw the rock-hard expression on his face and knew further protests were futile. She ran from the house, checking rooms for volunteers on her way to the door, but it appeared that most people had already left. Punching the numbers for help on her cell phone, she looked at the center and watched in horror as flames shot out of the back of the building.

Less than a moment later, a man pulled Rose out the front door. "My baby," she cried. "My baby. He's still in there."

A knot of dread formed in the back of Bella's throat. "Oh, no," she said, reaching out to Rose and taking the sobbing woman into her arms.

Sirens shrieked in the distance. Bella glanced toward the building. Where was Michael?

"I have to go back," Rose said. "I can't lose him."

"You can't," Bella said, wishing she could go in and look for the boy. "You need to be waiting for him when he comes out."

Rose looked at her with tear-stained eyes. "But what if he doesn't come out? It was so smoky in there. I could hardly breathe."

A slice of fear for Michael's safety cut through her. Why was he still in there? The sirens grew louder as the first red truck pulled in front of the center. Another explosion roared from the back of the house. The volunteers standing outside yelled "No!"

Bella felt her stomach dip to her feet. What if Michael—

Smoke billowed through the front door as the firemen opened it. Michael, coughing hard, stepped outside with a small child in his arms. His T-shirt covered with soot, he quickly stepped away from the building. A medic raced toward him.

"Rose," Bella said, emotion tightening her voice. "Rose, isn't that your son?" she asked, urging the woman to lift her head from her shoulder.

Rose glanced up and looked around. Spotting her son, she lifted her hand to her throat. "My baby. My baby," she said and ran toward him and the medic.

Filled with a range of emotions she couldn't begin to name, Bella watched Michael as he brushed off a medic. He glanced around the area and the second his gaze landed on her, she felt as if she'd been hit by a thunderbolt.

He moved toward her and she automatically did the same. She looked him over, taking in scrapes and burn marks. He covered a cough. "Come on. I don't want you around this."

"Me?" she said. "I've been outside just watching. You're the one who stayed in there too long."

"I heard that boy calling and couldn't figure out where he was. I went in every room. I finally tried the closets. There he was. Everyone accounted for?"

"I hope so," she said and looked around. The crowd around the center was growing. "There's the volunteer coordinator. Looks like she's checking off a list." The woman glanced at her and gave a quick wave.

Michael took her hand. "Let's make sure everyone is accounted for." After Michael double-checked everyone's safety, he answered questions from the police and fire department.

"We can go now," he said.

"Don't you think you should let the medic take a look at you?"

"No," he said. "The press will be here any minute."

"Are you afraid of the press?" she asked.

"No," he said with a scowl. "But I like my privacy."

She studied him for a long moment, taking in his discomfort and realization hit her. "You don't want them to know you were a hero."

He scoffed. "I wasn't a hero. I just heard a screaming kid and dragged him out of the place."

"A burning building," she corrected. "And you really should see a medic."

"Enough," he said, tugging her with him. "Since you're so concerned about my injuries, you can take care of them when we get home."

"What about my car?" she asked as he led her to his SUV.

"I'll send one of my drivers to collect it," he said and stuffed her inside.

An hour later, after Michael had taken a shower, wincing as the water sluiced over his scrapes and burns, he wrapped a towel around his waist and walked into his bedroom to the sight of Bella standing beside his bed. She must have showered also because her hair was damp and she'd changed clothes.

She gestured toward the bed and he noticed she'd placed a sheet on top of his bedspread.

"You have plans for me?" he asked, his body quickening despite his soreness.

She lifted a tube and a small bottle. "Antibiotic ointment for your boo-boos and eucalyptus oil for your massage." She turned on a CD that played soothing sounds of nature and gentle tones.

"Massage," he said in approval.

"I'm not licensed, but I've learned a little on my

own." She waved her hand briskly. "On the bed," she commanded.

"Sounds like an order," he said reclining.

"It was," she said, a smile playing over her lips as she studied his face and began to dab ointment on his scrapes. She slid her hands over his shoulders, arms and hands, making hmm sounds.

Michael was accustomed to having a woman's sexual attention, but Bella's tender touch seemed to reach deeper than his skin. When was the last time someone besides himself had taken care of his scrapes? He couldn't remember. Why did it matter? As she began to rub the fragrant oil into his shoulders, he felt as if a stream of water was trickling through parts of him left dry and abandoned for ages. He wasn't sure he liked the sensation.

He watched her brow furrow as she worked his right shoulder from the front. "Are you always this tense?"

He winced when she hit a sore spot. "I had to pull off the door to the closet. It was stuck."

She pursed her lips in disapproval. "You didn't mention that. Anything else I should know?"

"No. Why are you doing this?" he asked, studying the intent expression on her face.

"Because it needs to be done and you wouldn't take the time for it." He was a complex man, she thought. Far more complicated than she'd suspected. Full of layers that made her curious. She wondered about his secrets as she rubbed his shoulders.

"There's a difference between need and want."

She put her hand over his mouth. "Be quiet. I need to concentrate." She turned back to the massage.

"Are you saying my talking distracts you?"

"Your voice is—" She broke off, sinking her fingers

into his muscles, causing him to moan. She smiled at the sound. "Good spot?"

He nodded. "My voice is?"

"Compelling," she said. "Well, *you* are compelling, but you already knew that."

"How so?" he asked, curious because she clearly wasn't flattering him.

"You're insufferably confident and intelligent. You seem intent on conveying that you only make decisions based on numbers and that you're nearly heartless. But you're not. There's stuff going on beneath the surface. Not exactly sure—" She dug her thumbs into the muscle above his collarbone and he winced. "Oops. Good or bad?"

"I'm okay," he said.

She smiled. "You really need to let me know if I hurt you. If you don't, you're going to need to take something for your muscles later."

He didn't believe her. She was a small woman. He'd suffered more than a massage without needing medication. "I'm okay."

"All righty," she said and slid her hand over his face. "Close your eyes," she said softly. She worked his shoulders, arms, and even his hands. After he turned over, she continued and he wondered how she kept from tiring. Her fingers played him with a soothing rhythm of increasing and decreasing intensity.

Michael relaxed in a way he couldn't recall, feeling himself melt into the mattress. He drifted off....

Later, he awakened to the sound of the CD she'd played while she'd massaged his body. A light sheet covered him. Lifting his head, he glanced around and felt a tug of disappointment that she was gone. A bottle of water caught his eye. Sighing, he rose and grabbed it, spotting a note next to it.

Gone to check on Charlotte. Drink lots of water. Jacuzzi would be a good follow-up to the massage. Be back later.

More orders, he thought, lifting his eyebrows. Few women had tried to give him orders. Those who had hadn't lasted long. At the moment, though, he couldn't help feeling indulgent. Bella had taken him to a new level of relaxation. He would take them both to a new level of sexual pleasure.

He decided to follow her suggestion for a dip in the Jacuzzi. But first he should check his BlackBerry for messages. He picked up his phone from the nightstand, noting that she'd turned it off. Only he controlled his phone. He would warn her later.

Turning it on, he saw a text message from his private investigator and immediately called him.

"Sam Carson," the man said his name. "Is this Mr. Medici?"

"Yes. You have news."

"Yes, but you aren't going to like it."

Michael's gut twisted. "What is it? Did you find his body?"

Carson sighed. "That would have been easier than what I have to tell you."

Eight

Michael's house was dark when Bella let herself in just before nine o'clock. Normally she would have expected one of his staff to greet her, but this time all she heard was silence. Was he still asleep from the massage she'd given him?

Turning on a light, she walked through the hallway to the kitchen and glimpsed a flicker of light coming from the den. The gas fireplace provided the only light in the room. It took a moment for her eyes to adjust. She saw him sitting in a chair holding a squat glass half-full of liquid. Probably some kind of liquor that cost a hundred dollars an ounce.

She met his gaze and glimpsed a turbulence in his gaze. Something had happened since she'd left. "What's wrong?" she asked, moving toward him.

"Nothing I want to discuss," he said and took a sip of his drink. "Do you want anything to drink?"

She lifted her bottle of water. "I'm good."

"Yes, you are," he said, seduction glinting in his eyes.

Uncertain of his mood, she stopped a few steps before him. "Are you okay?"

"I am," he said, but his words belied her instincts.

"You really should still be drinking water," she said. "Did you get into the Jacuzzi?"

"No more orders today, Bella. And no, I didn't get into the hot tub. Come here."

She moved closer, still hesitant. He extended his hand and she accepted it. He pulled her into his lap, his gaze pinning hers. "Don't ever, ever turn off my Blackberry without my permission."

She blinked. "You missed an important call," she said. "I'm sorry," she said. "Kinda," she added. "Kinda not. You needed to relax."

"That's not your decision to make."

"Okay. I don't suppose you want to tell me about the call," she ventured.

"You supposed correctly."

"But I can tell you've got something on your mind. Something is bothering you," she said.

He set his glass on the table beside him and pulled her mouth to his. "Give me something else to think about."

His mouth devoured hers while his hands slid over her, immediately making her hot. She sensed a dark desperation beneath the surface, but she wasn't sure what it was. He distracted her from dwelling on it with the speed and intensity of his lovemaking. Before she knew it, her clothes had been discarded and so had his.

On the floor in front of the fireplace, he took her entire

body with his hands and his mouth. His gaze holding hers with the firelight dancing over his skin, he thrust inside her.

Bella gasped at the feeling of possession. With each stroke, she felt utterly and completely consumed, falling under some kind of spell he cast over her. It couldn't be love, she told herself. Love was gentle and sweet and this was nothing like that. This was compelling and powerful, but complicated. And temporary.

Temporary, she repeated to herself like a mantra. *Temporary.* But it was hard to convince herself of that when she'd never had a man make love to her with such power as Michael. Their arrangement had been about sex, but something else was happening between them.

The next morning, Bella awakened in Michael's bed. As usual, he was gone. Exercising, she guessed and crept out of bed. She pulled on a robe from his closet and walked down the hallway to his small, well-equipped gym. The door was open and she spotted him on the elliptical, moving at a fast pace, his arms gleaming with perspiration. His gaze fixed forward, he looked as if he were racing against the devil. It occurred to her for all Michael's ability to make ruthless business decisions and his tendency to avoid emotional interaction, he had his demons. The strangest, craziest desire to rid him of those demons sprang inside her.

Insane, she thought. As if she had the power to help him. As if he would even want her help.

Bella didn't have time to dwell on her conflicted feelings for Michael. Her aunt's spa opened, and she and her aunt were busy accommodating the surge of customers.

"You have to hire more people," Bella said to Charlotte after the first week. "It's part of your agreement with Michael."

"I know, I know," Charlotte said as she sank into a chair. "I just didn't dream we'd get this kind of response. Michael was right about creating miniservices that give people a taste of luxury without spending too much."

"And we've sold several discount packages for pedicures and massages," Bella added, and gave Charlotte a glass of iced green tea. "So, when are you going to hire new staff?"

"I'll talk to Michael to confirm. I don't want to mess up this time," she said. "I don't want to overhire either."

"But you also don't want to over*tire,*" Bella said.

"Hear, hear," a male voice said from the doorway. Fred, a man in his fifties who worked at the computer store down the street, popped in daily for a visit.

Charlotte perked up. "I thought the sign on the door said closed," she teased.

"Not for your best customer," Fred said with a twinkle in his eye.

"Customer," Charlotte said. "You haven't spent a dime on any services here. You just show up after work and drink my coffee and waste my time."

Bella smiled at the dynamics between them. Charlotte might not admit it, but she clearly enjoyed Fred's attention.

"Then how about if I change that?" he asked. "Can I take an overworked owner manager to dinner tonight in Buckhead?"

Charlotte blinked, clearly speechless. "Uh, well." She cleared her throat. "That's very nice of you, but I still have a lot of work to do. Go over the day's book-keeping and supplies."

"I can do that," Bella offered.

Charlotte glared at her. "Don't you have plans with Michael?"

"No. He's actually out of town," she said. Michael had been out of town most of the week. She'd spent her nights feeling alternately full of relief and missing him. The latter had surprised her. After all, wasn't their relationship just supposed to be physical?

"Well, I don't know," Charlotte said, still reluctant.

"I did have a question about a couple of the products we're using. They're in the supply closet," Bella said then glanced at Fred. "Could you excuse us for a moment? We'll be right back."

Bella took her aunt's hand and led her to the walk-in supply closet and closed the door. "Why won't you go to dinner with him? It's obvious that he likes you," she whispered.

"I have too much work to do," Charlotte protested. "Plus, he didn't give me any notice. Just wandered in here and assumed I'd be willing to go." She ran her fingers through her hair nervously. Although her hair was still short, her aunt looked stylish and attractive. "It's probably just a pity request."

"Pity request," Bella said with a snort. "Is that why he stops in here every afternoon and sometimes at lunch?"

"Maybe he just likes the free coffee and cookies," Charlotte said.

"That's why he wants to take you some place really

nice," Bella said, rolling her eyes. "Because he wants to pay you back for coffee and cookies."

"Why are you pushing me?"

"Because I think you like him and maybe he would be good to you. You deserve to have someone who is good to you."

Charlotte sighed. "I just don't know. I'd given up on anything with a man."

"Maybe you gave up too soon," Bella said.

Charlotte tapped her fingernails on a shelf. "You really think I should go?"

"Yes!"

She frowned, studying Bella for a long moment. "How are you and Michael doing? You don't say very much about him."

"There's not much to say. We're getting to know each other."

"Are you starting to get over Stephen?"

Bella felt her stomach clench and turned away. "I don't—" She broke off. "It's a different kind of relationship with Michael."

"In what way?" her aunt said, digging for information.

Bella shrugged. "Michael is just for fun," she said, nearly choking on the words as she said them. "Stephen and I were in love."

"You've been the kettle calling the pot black," her aunt said. "You're telling me to open the door and give Fred a chance. When are you going to give Michael a chance?"

Never, she thought. Instead, she smiled and wagged her finger at her aunt. "We're not going to turn this conversation on me. You need to freshen up and tell that man out there you'll join him for dinner."

* * *

Sitting in a penthouse suite in Chicago, Michael glanced at the invitation for the Valentine wine tasting at the exclusive historical Essex House and debated attending. It was mostly a social event, where Atlanta's elite would try to show each other up. He didn't give a damn about that, but The Essex House had recently courted him. He suspected they wanted him to invest and lend his name because their bottom line was sagging. The trouble was that he wouldn't have complete control, he would only have a vote in the management of the House, and that didn't appeal to him at all.

Still, turning The Essex House into a financial success was seductive, another challenge.

The word *challenge* brought Bella to mind. In fact, she'd been on his mind more often than ever lately. Yes, she knew how to burn up his bed, but she got under his skin in other ways. Those violet eyes of hers seemed to see right through him at times. He knew such a thing wasn't possible, but that didn't stop him from wondering….

He glanced at the invitation again and made a decision. He picked up his cell and dialed Bella.

"Hi. How's the Windy City?" she asked, clearly reading her caller ID.

"Windy and cold," he said. "What are you doing?"

"Some work for my aunt. She's out to dinner with a *man*," she said, the shocked delight in her voice making him smile.

"You sound surprised," he said.

"She's always been such a workaholic. She was married and divorced for a while before she took me in.

She dated every now and then, but nothing serious and nothing in the last few years. A man who works down the street wanted to take her to Buckhead and she almost refused. I had to prod her to go out." Bella laughed. "So she's eating a gourmet meal and I'm eating gourmet jelly beans."

"You could call my chef and have him bring you something," he offered.

"That's okay. I really don't mind. How's your work going?"

"Good," he said. "I'll be back in town tomorrow morning and need to attend an event tomorrow night. I'd like you to join me," he said.

"What is it?"

The wariness in her voice irritated him. "The Valentine wine tasting at The Essex House."

Silence followed.

"Bella," he prompted.

"The Essex House? Isn't the wine tasting one of those events that's featured on television and in the newspaper?"

"Yes, and national magazines. It begins at seven. You can either get ready at my house earlier—"

"Whoa, I didn't say I could go. For one thing, that's making our relationship way too public. I told you I didn't want that."

"Why are you so concerned about that?"

"Because I don't want to have to explain things after we're finished," she said.

His irritation tightened further. "It's not that big a deal."

"Maybe not to you. What am I supposed to say? That you and I had a sexual arrangement and now it's over?"

He narrowed his eyes. "Our arrangement is for an affair. An affair includes other activities. If you're that worried about what to say after we're finished, just tell people you dumped me."

Bella gave a short laugh. "Right," she said. "As if anyone would believe that."

"Why not?"

"Because women don't usually dump handsome, rich bachelors."

"You can be the exception," he said. "If you're not at my house by six, I'll pick you up at your apartment at six-thirty. Enjoy your jelly—"

"Wait!"

"What?"

"I don't have anything to wear," she confessed in a low voice.

"Pick something out tomorrow. I'll pay for it. I'll send my driver over with my credit card."

"I have to work tomorrow. Saturday is our busiest day."

"Make good use of your lunch break then," he said without budging an inch.

She gave a sigh. "You are so bossy. It would serve you right if I maxed out your card."

He laughed. "Sweetheart, give it a try. You couldn't do that in a year, let alone one day."

After a busy morning at the spa, Bella headed straight for the shopping district. She was uncomfortable using Michael's money for her clothing, but there was no way around it. She visited several high-end shops, but nothing felt right. Accepting his money to purchase her clothing just seemed to remind her how much she wished she could help her aunt on her own. On a whim, she went into a vintage shop and found a black, beaded, chiffon flapper-style dress she could pair with black boots and a silk scarf. The style was more funky luxe than strictly luxurious, but it suited her and didn't cost the earth.

If Michael didn't like it, then perhaps he wouldn't take her out in public again, she thought deviously. She worked the rest of the afternoon and scooted out an hour early to get ready. She would never admit to the surge of excitement and anticipation sizzling inside her.

Ridiculous, she thought as she lined her eyes and applied red lipstick. The event would just be a group of stuffy society types. Her doorbell rang and her heart lurched. Michael's driver. Grab scarf, purse and coat, she reminded herself. "Just a minute," she called.

Collecting her things, she opened the door to Michael, drop-dead gorgeous in a tux. Her breath whooshed out of her lungs. "Oh, I didn't expect you."

He lifted his eyebrow. "Who, then?"

"The driver," she said, feeling his gaze travel over her from head to toe.

"You—" He hesitated a second and his mouth lifted in a half grin. "Sparkle."

Pleasure rushed through her. "Thank you. I didn't do too much damage to your card."

"I told you I wasn't worried about it." He glanced beyond her to her apartment. "This is where you live?"

"Yes," she said, trying not to feel self-conscious. Her apartment probably could serve as a closet in the home. "It's small, but cozy."

"It's not the safest neighborhood," he said.

"Neighbors here watch out for each other. I'm okay with it," she said stiffly and stepped into the hallway.

"I wasn't criticizing," he said.

"Your house is much more luxurious, but I'm happy to have a little space of my own."

"You say that as if you think I've always lived like I do now," he chided, closing the space between them. "You know where I came from."

"Looking at you in that tux, it's easy to forget," she said.

"Don't," he said. "One of the things I like about you is that you're not overly impressed by my wealth."

"So you *like* me disagreeable?" she asked. "Does this mean I should tell you I've decided not to attend the wine tasting?"

He took her hand in his. "Not a chance. Besides, I can tell you want to go."

She gave a mock sniff. "I read about it in the newspaper. They are supposed to serve some good desserts, so that should make it worthwhile."

Michael ushered her to his limo and the driver whisked them to The Essex House. The carefully tended mansion buzzed with activity. Crystal chandeliers lit the gleaming marble floors and antique furniture. The sound of a piano playing romantic standards in another room wafted through the house. With her fingers linked in Michael's, she almost felt like this was a real date.

"What do you think?" he asked.

"It's beautiful. It reminds me of a high-class woman from the 1800s. The place seems to have a personality of its own."

"Excellent description," he said. "Maintaining a high-class woman is expensive."

Bella couldn't help wondering if he felt the same

way about his relationship with her. The notion threatened to sour her pleasure, so she quickly brushed it aside. "Good thing they continue to make enough money to do the job."

"We'll see," he said with a sliver of doubt in his voice.

"What do you mean? Are they in trouble?" she asked.

"They've asked me to invest both my money and my expertise, but the collective board votes on final decisions."

She watched him studying the house and staff. "Does that mean you wouldn't get to rule?" she asked and shook her head. "Good luck to them."

He chuckled. "We'll see. At least I'm here."

"I should have known this involved business," she muttered, wondering why she felt let down. Why should she care that Michael was motivated by business for the evening? Sure, it was Valentine's Day and many other couples might view it as a romantic affair, but she shouldn't.

"You sound disappointed," he said, searching her face.

Embarrassed that he'd read her so easily, she shook her head. "There's still dessert," she said, forcing a smile.

A balding man approached Michael at that moment, earning her a reprieve. "Mr. Medici, I'm Clarence Kiddlow. We spoke on the phone. I'm glad you decided to attend. We're the hottest ticket in town tonight," the man said proudly.

Michael nodded. "Mr. Kiddlow, this is my date, Bella St. Clair."

Clarence extended his hand. "My pleasure to meet

you." He waved toward a server. "Have some wine," he said. "We're starting with a white from Virginia of all places. But it's very smooth." He turned to Michael after he'd tasted the wine. "What do you think?"

"Bella is the white-wine drinker. What do you think?"

Surprised he'd deferred to her, she nodded. "Very nice, thank you."

The server then poured her a full glass.

"I'd like to show you around and tell you about some of our plans," Clarence said. "I think you'll find them interesting."

"Thank you," Michael said. "Later, perhaps. Bella and I would like to look around on our own first."

Surprise crossed Clarence's face, but he acquiesced. "Of course. Tell me when you're ready."

Bella felt surprise of her own as Michael ushered her away. "I thought you were here to investigate the possibility of working with The Essex House."

"I didn't come for a sales presentation," he said, impatience flitting across his face. "I'm not an idiot. Given the choice between Clarence's company and yours, which do you think I would choose?"

Bella blinked and fought a rush of pleasure. "I don't know what to say. The mighty Michael Medici just paid me a compliment."

"Don't let it go to your head," he said and led her through a crowded hallway. He nodded in the direction of a room to the left. "I think I've spotted what you're looking for."

"A delicious dessert, but I wonder, Michael, what are you looking for?" she couldn't resist asking.

He turned back to her, giving her a second and

third glance. "I have everything I need and more. If I want something else, I find a way to get it. You should know that."

Her stomach dipped at the expression on his face. "I suppose I should, but I was speaking of dessert."

He smiled. "I'll enjoy watching you have yours. Come on," he said and tugged her into the room. The throng around the serving table made it difficult to get close. "Wait here," he said and positioned her in a corner. "I'll get it for you."

She watched him walk away and wondered how he managed to part the crowd with such ease. It was as if they knew they should defer to him. Bella wondered if his tough upbringing had instilled him with that quality. She couldn't deny that he fascinated her. She wanted to know more about him. She wasn't in love with him and never would be, but she cared about him far more than she'd planned. She wasn't sure how that had happened.

A moment later, Michael appeared, carrying a plateful of the most decadent dessert Bella had even seen in her life. She looked at him and the chocolate and wondered if he had any idea how much he had in common with that treat. Decadent and forbidden, both could cause a woman to pay for indulging.

He approached her and lifted a spoonful to her lips. "Tell me what you think of it," he said.

Nine

Accepting the dare in his gaze, but telling herself it wasn't at all significant, Bella opened her mouth and slowly savored a bite of the decadent dessert. "Now, that is good," she said, reaching for the spoon. "Really good."

Michael playfully pulled the spoon from her reach. "Not so fast."

She met his gaze and scowled at him. "No teasing allowed."

"That's the pot calling the kettle black. You're a walking tease."

She fought his flattery. After all, it wasn't necessary given their arrangement. "Hand over the chocolate and no one will get hurt," she threatened.

He chuckled and lifted the spoon to her mouth again. She took it, but a familiar face shot into view. The chocolate stuck in her throat as she stared into her ex-fiancé's eyes.

"Bella?" Stephen said, clearly shocked to see her at such an event. His new fiancée came into Bella's view and the two wound through the crowd.

Her stomach gave a vicious turn.

"Bella, what are you doing here?" Stephen asked, then looked at Michael and gave a double take. "Michael Medici," he said.

Britney smiled broadly. "Michael, it's great to see you again. We met a couple years ago at the heart disease charity dinner."

Michael nodded and glanced at Stephen. "And this is?"

"Stephen, my fiancé." She giggled. "We've set the date for our wedding in August. We would love for you to come. You know my father thinks so highly of you."

"Send him my best," Michael said. "How do you know Bella?"

"I could ask the same," Stephen said, glancing from the chocolate dessert in Michael's hand to Bella.

Bella felt a rush of self-consciousness. "Stephen and I met in college."

"Ah," Michael said and turned to Steven. "Bella and I met through business."

"Really?" Stephen said. "Bella and business?"

"I've been working with my aunt in her spa."

"Oh, I thought she had some problems…" Stephen said, faltering under Michael's hard gaze.

"She did, but the business is now booming," Michael said. "Best wishes on your marriage. Don't let us keep you from the event." His dismissive tone quickly sent the couple on their way.

"Thank you very much," Britney said.

As soon as they left, Michael turned to Bella. "What's the real story about Stephen?"

She swallowed over the bitterness in the back of her throat. "Water over the bridge, under the dam, whatever. Old news. I wonder what the next kind of wine will be," she said, skirting his gaze. "Let's go—"

Michael caught her hand. "Bella, I have excellent instincts and my instincts tell me you're holding out on me."

"Well, it's not the best kind of story for this venue. Can we please just shelve this and enjoy the rest of the evening?" she asked.

"The question is *can* you shelve it?"

"Since this is probably the only time I'll be at The Essex House, I'm going to give it a damn good try," she said.

A sliver of approval shot through his dark eyes. "Okay. Let's see about that wine."

Michael successfully kept Bella away from Britney and Stephen. It wasn't difficult. The Essex House was packed. He noticed men taking long glances at Bella throughout the evening. He also noticed that Bella didn't notice. She was too busy taking in her surroundings, reading the biographies of the ancestors who'd built and occupied the house.

She sipped wine and sampled little bites of the desserts, but her whole demeanor seemed muted since their interaction with Stephen. Again, he wondered about the two of them. He knew they'd been lovers and the knowledge made him burn with surprising jealousy. Michael had never thought of himself as the possessive type. He couldn't recall any other woman who'd inspired the hot coal of jealousy in his gut.

Why should he care about her romantic history now?

He knew she was attracted to him. She couldn't fake the sensual response she gave him in bed. She was his for now, for as long as he wanted her. That was the bargain.

Suddenly, the way he'd persuaded her to accept her attraction to him made him feel vaguely dissatisfied. Given the choice, she would have denied herself and him. From the beginning, though, he'd known they should be together until the passion between them became less intense, until it burned away.

He watched her cover a yawn. "Ready to go?"

She gave a wry smile. "I guess the day is catching up with me. Maybe you should go see the man who greeted us. He's going to be disappointed if he doesn't get a chance to talk with you further tonight."

"He's a big boy. He'll get over it."

"But you came for business purposes. Don't you want to talk with him?"

"Not tonight. I'll page the chauffeur to pick us up. It won't take but a moment." He ushered her toward the front door and they collected her wrap.

The limo appeared just as they walked down the front steps. Once inside, she leaned her head against the back of the seat, closed her eyes and sighed. He pulled an ice-cold bottle of water from the ice bucket, lifted her hand and wrapped her fingers around the bottle.

She opened her eyes and blinked, then smiled. "Thank you."

"You're welcome. You want to tell me about you and Stephen now?" he asked. "You turned as white as a sheet when he showed up."

"I could remind you that you wouldn't tell me what was bothering you that night you were sitting in the dark by the fire," she said.

"You could, but it wouldn't be wise," he said.

"So, you're allowed to have your touchy subject, but I'm not allowed to have mine?" she countered. "You don't have to discuss yours. I don't have to discuss mine."

Frustration stabbed at him. He wasn't accustomed to being pushed back with such nonchalance. "You could have fainted. I should have had a heads-up so I could take care of you."

"We have an arrangement, remember? You don't need to take care of me. You can't do anything about this anyway. No one can."

The despondence on her face ripped at him. "How do you know I can't do anything about it?"

Her eyes turned shiny with unshed tears. "Stephen and I were going to be married. He fell in love with someone else and now he's going to marry her." Her voice broke. "See? What could anyone do about that."

Michael stared at her, feeling a sick, sinking sensation in his gut. His reaction surprised him. "You're still in love with him, aren't you?"

She closed her eyes and he watched as one telltale tear traveled down her cheek.

It shouldn't bother him. Their relationship was primarily physical. He avoided emotional scenes like the plague. The fact, however, that the woman who'd shared his bed for the last few weeks was in love with another man bothered the hell out of him.

He lifted his hand to her face and rubbed his finger over her wet cheek. He looked into her sad eyes. "He chose unwisely. Britney will drive him up a tree with that shrill voice of hers."

Her lips twitched with a flash of humor then she closed her eyes again releasing another tear. Filled with a crazy combination of emotions, he pulled her into his arms. "If he gave you up, then he's not worthy of you."

She took a shaky breath as if she were trying to compose herself. "Easy to say. My heart says something different."

"What does your heart say?"

She lifted her gaze to his. "He was the one."

He felt as if she'd stabbed him in the gut. His pride quickly rose in defense. "If he was the one, if you were in love with him, why did you agree to an affair with me?"

She looked away. "I'd already messed up my chance for my future, and I'd let down my aunt by not being here when she was so ill. If I agreed to your bargain, I could at least make things right for Charlotte."

"And desire had nothing to do with it," he said in disbelief. "You hated every minute you spent in my bed."

She bit her lip. "I didn't say that." She lifted her gaze reluctantly. "I can't deny there's a strong passion between you and me, but I knew it wasn't love."

He'd gotten exactly what he'd wanted. Her passion with no emotional complications. Why was it suddenly not enough?

Michael didn't sleep with her that night or the next. Bella wondered if he'd changed his mind about her. About them. If he didn't want her anymore. She felt a strange combination of relief and emptiness at his absence.

His passion had been so consuming she found it hard to breathe, let alone think. Without him, she was left with her own thoughts and feelings. Her own loss.

Running from her pain, she worked overtime at the spa to keep herself busy. She went in early and left late wondering if Michael would abandon his support of the spa since his interest in her had waned. He, too, left the house early and didn't return until late. After the fourth night of this routine, she decided to sleep at her apartment instead of his house. Perhaps he wouldn't notice. Perhaps she would be able to sleep better if she wasn't in the same house.

At ten o'clock, a knock sounded at her door. Startled, she muted the basketball game she'd been half watching and ran to her door to look through the peephole. Her heart dipped. Michael stood outside, and even from this microview of him, she could see his impatience.

She opened the door.

"Why are you here?" he asked and strode inside, closing the door behind him.

"Um, well I've been working late at the spa and you've been working late, so I just thought I would sleep here tonight."

His gaze felt like a laser trained on her. "Is that all?"

She cleared her throat, finding his scrutiny nearly unbearable. "Well, we haven't really—" She swallowed.

He lifted an eyebrow. "Really what?"

"Um. Talked."

"You were very upset after the incident at The Essex House. I thought I should give you some time."

Surprised at his consideration, she stared. "Oh. That was thoughtful."

He shot her a wry half smile. "You sound shocked," he said, then waved his hand when she opened her mouth to respond. "No need to defend yourself. Mind if I stay awhile?"

Surprise after surprise. "Uh, no. Would you like something to drink? I don't have much," she quickly added.

"Beer?" he asked as he pulled off his leather jacket and sat down.

"Sorry, no. Water, juice and soda."

"Water's good." He looked at the TV. "You're watching the Hawks. How are they doing?"

Bella pulled two bottles of water from the refrigerator and put a bag of popcorn in the microwave. "You tell me."

"Up by five. Not bad. I didn't know you were a fan."

The microwave dinged and she poured the popcorn into a bowl. "I have a new appreciation for Atlanta sports. I missed them when I was out of the country."

He nodded. "Ever seen them live?"

She shook her head as she joined him on the sofa.

"I'll have to take you sometime," he said.

She almost asked *why,* but managed to stop herself. This was a different side of Michael, one she'd glimpsed before that first night together when the two of them had shared casual conversation and she hadn't known what a workaholic he was. So much had happened since that night that it now seemed ages ago.

They ate popcorn and watched the game. When it was over, Michael turned off the TV and met her gaze.

A familiar, but forbidden ripple of anticipation curled in her belly. She'd seen that look in his eyes often enough to know what happened next. He would take her to bed and for a short time make her forget everything but the passion they shared.

Leaning closer and closer until his mouth took hers, he kissed her with a lover's knowledge of what pleased her. Her body grew warm under his caress. She wanted closer. She wanted more.

He deepened the kiss and she felt herself sinking,

drinking in his taste and scent, feeling the ripple of the muscles of his arms beneath her fingertips. Her body buzzed with want.

He pulled away. She felt the tension inside him. Reluctance and need emanated from him. His eyes glinted with passion. "I had a good time. I'll see you tomorrow," he said and rose.

Bella watched in shock as he pulled on his jacket. Her knees still weak from the promise of his passion, she stiffened them and stood. "Tomorrow?" she echoed.

"Yeah, I'll call you. Lock the door behind me. Okay?"

She mutely nodded and watched him walk away. *What was going on?*

Michael called her the following day, but he didn't ask to see her. More confused than ever, she stayed late again at the Spa.

"You should leave," her aunt said. "You've been working too hard lately."

"No, I haven't," Bella said. "Business is booming and I'm here to make sure *you* don't work too hard."

"Well, you can only do inventory so many times before you wear the labels off the products." Charlotte narrowed her eyes as she studied her. "I haven't seen Michael the last few days."

Determined not to squirm beneath her aunt's scrutiny, Bella wandered to the front desk and unnecessarily tidied it. "He's very busy. You know he's always got a deal going."

"Hmm," Charlotte said and moved closer. "Are you still seeing each other?"

"Sure, I saw him last night. He came over and watched the basketball game," Bella said.

"Hmm," Charlotte said again. "There's something you're not telling me. Something's not right."

"Everything is fine," Bella insisted. "Everything is great. My wonderful aunt is thriving and even dating. The spa is doing great. I couldn't be more pleased."

"And maybe if you keep saying it, you'll believe it yourself," Charlotte said and took Bella's hand. "I'm worried about you. You've sacrificed your professional plans for me."

"What plans?" Bella asked. "Besides, I got to pursue my dreams last year. It's your turn now."

Charlotte's brow furrowed. "I don't want you to be unhappy. Are you still hung up on Stephen?"

Bella tried, but for a flash of a second, she couldn't conceal her feelings. "Stephen has moved on. You know that."

"And you need to do the same," Charlotte urged. "Don't you like Michael?"

Like, Bella thought. As if such a tame emotion could ever apply to the man.

"He's done so much for us," Charlotte continued. "And he's so handsome. Doesn't he treat you well?"

"Of course he does," Bella said. "Michael is just a different kind of man than Stephen."

"Darn right he is," Charlotte said. "He's a leader, not a follower. And if you want him, you're going to have to give him a run for his money."

Bella blinked. "Excuse me?"

"I mean Michael Medici is worth exerting yourself, and I'm not talking about his money. You never had to exert yourself with Stephen. He was always there for you."

"Until I went away," Bella said, feeling a twinge.

"That's just your ego talking," Charlotte said.

Bella dropped her jaw in surprise. "That's not true. Stephen and I were very much in love."

Charlotte waved her hand, dismissing Bella's protest. "You need a man, not a boy. Who knows when Stephen will grow up and stand on his own? Michael Medici is your match. You just need to make sure he knows that."

A knock sounded and Charlotte looked at the door, a smile transforming her face. "Oh, that's Fred. He's taking me to a traveling production of *Wicked*." She walked toward the door. "You need to get out of here and have some fun. You're starting to act like an old lady." She threw Bella a kiss. "Good night, Sweetie."

Go after Michael? Bella shook her head. She wouldn't even know how to begin. Besides, she didn't want him. Not that way. Right? She certainly cared about him as a human being, and she was grateful for his help with her aunt's business. Her cheeks heated as she remembered their lovemaking. Yes, he was passionate, but he was also emotionally remote. That would never work for her. Bella wanted a man who wore his heart on his sleeve. That was not Michael.

Her cell phone rang and she glanced at the caller ID. Despite herself, her heart leapt. Irritated, she answered the phone. "Hi, Michael."

"I got tickets for a Hawks game tomorrow night. Wanna go?" he asked.

She wondered why he was asking. All the other times she'd been with him her presence had been required.

"If you don't, then—"

"No," she said. "I mean yes, I'd love to."

"Good, I'll pick you up at six. We can eat dinner first."

Click. She stared at her phone and chuckled to herself. *Yeah, now that's a guy who wears his heart on his sleeve. Not.* So why was she already planning what to wear?

Ten

The limo whisked Bella and Michael to the restaurant and he led her inside. She noticed that he barely mentioned his name before the host escorted them to a table with a view of the lighted fountain in the center of the restaurant. Seconds later, a waiter appeared and took their wine order.

"I've heard about this place. It's beautiful."

"A bit theatrical," he said. "Not bad, though. I've been trying to hire the chef away for years."

"And the mighty Michael Medici has been unsuccessful?" she teased.

He shot her a mock dark glare. "The chef is married to the owner's daughter."

She laughed. "I guess that could make it a bit more challenging. I'm surprised you didn't just buy the restaurant out from under the owner."

"I tried," Michael admitted. "Anthony is a true restauranteur. He'll be doing this forever."

"And you admire him?"

"Yeah. He came up the hard way. Not the same way I did. But he had it tough."

The waiter appeared and took their food order. Midway through their meal, a portly middle-aged gentleman approached their table. "You are enjoying your dinner?" the man asked.

Michael rose. "Delicious, Anthony. I know where to take someone I want to impress."

Anthony laughed and clasped Michael's hand with both of his. "You are too kind. No matter what you say, I will not sell."

Michael sighed. "I had to try. The lady here is quite impressed. Bella St. Clair, may I present Anthony Garfield."

Anthony turned to her and extended his hand. "*Bella*, Bella. I can see why you would want to bring her to my restaurant. Such a woman doesn't deserve second best."

"You're too kind," Bella said. "Your restaurant is fabulous."

Michael cocked his head to one side. "You're not referring to my restaurants, are you Anthony?" Michael said, sending Bella a knowing glance.

Anthony shrugged and his eyes twinkled with competitive humor. "I would never say that. I've sent several of my customers to you."

"When you were already booked," Michael said.

"As you have done to me," Anthony said. "You're a master competitor, but you need to be kept on your toes."

"And you're just the man to do it. A great dining experience."

"Thank you. High praise from such a man." He turned to Bella. "You keep him in line, okay?"

Me? Bella opened her mouth. "I'm not sure it's possible to keep Michael in line."

Anthony gave a quick nod. "Every man has his Waterloo. Good evening to both of you."

Michael sat down. "We trade top restaurant pick every other year. As much as I hate getting second place to anyone, I don't mind as much to him."

"He seems to respect you, too," she said. "I'm surprised you didn't take me to one of your restaurants."

"Didn't you hear me say that I know where to take someone I want to impress?" he asked.

She met his gaze, feeling lightning race through her. He couldn't possibly want to impress her. She wasn't that important to him. And if she were... Why did the air seem to squeeze out of her lungs?

They left the restaurant and the limo drove them to Phillips Arena. Michael led her to a private box with an unbeatable view of the court.

She looked at him. "I guess I shouldn't ask how you managed this."

"I have standing box seats. I often give them away to VIP clients," he said.

"I don't know what to say."

"How about go Hawks?" he said and she felt another ripple race through her.

Throughout the game, she was super-conscious of every time he touched her. First her shoulder, then her hand. His thigh rubbed against hers, distracting her from the game. Once, he slid his hand behind the nape of her neck, and she could have sworn she felt sparkles down her back.

The game ended far too early, and before she knew it they were in the limo again.

"Do you want a nightcap, or are you ready to go back to your apartment?" he asked.

Frustration twisted through her. He had confused the living daylights out of her. A heavy sigh poured from her.

"Problem?" he asked.

She bit her lip, wondering if she should say anything. Wondering if she could. "Do you not want me anymore?" she blurted out.

He held her gaze for a long moment that made her stomach knot. He took her hand and slid his fingers sensually through hers. "Not want you? What makes you say that?"

In for a penny. In for a pound. "Because we haven't been together in days. And you were ready to leave me at my apartment tonight."

He paused again. "I want you willing. I want you wanting me. Or not at all."

Whoa. Bella's mind reeled with his words. He wasn't going to require her to be with him? What about their deal? What about her debt to him?

She stared into his dark eyes and felt as if her inner core was shifting. This was her chance to turn away and brush her hands of him. She could go back to her apartment and lick her wounds as long as she wanted. She could buy Ben & Jerry's ice cream and eat it every night. By herself.

Or, she could be with the most exciting man she'd ever met in her life. Even though she didn't love him. Suddenly she felt as if she were a runaway train on a track she had to take. At some point, there would be a terrible crash, but for some reason she couldn't miss being with him.

"Are you saying that you would continue to support my aunt's business even if you and I never see each other again?"

"Yes."

Her heart stopped. She took a deep breath. "Take me home," she said. "With you."

Michael did take her, in more ways than one. He didn't give her a chance to change her mind. As soon as they arrived at his house, he led her upstairs to the big bed where she'd been absent too long and made love to her. He relished the scent of her body and devoured every inch of her. He drowned himself in the softness of her skin and the passion that roared beneath.

He didn't want to think about how much he'd missed her, how much he'd wanted her. How had she become such an addiction? Her spirit, her emotions got under his skin. He still felt jealous of Stephen. It was an insane emotion, but he wanted to wipe away every memory of her former fiancé. He wanted her to think only of him. He wanted her to want only him.

Where had these feelings come from? He didn't want to feel this need for her, this deeper-than-his-bones connection with her.

The next morning, he loathed leaving her. The realization bothered him, but he brushed it aside and did his usual workout. After he finished, he noticed a message on his BlackBerry. He listened to it, feeling amused and irritated. Rafe was flying his wife and son, their brother Damien and his wife, to Atlanta this afternoon. Nothing like short notice.

Michael returned to his bedroom to find Bella sleeping in his bed. A fierce possessiveness filled him, but he fought it. This would pass, he told himself. No one had ever belonged to him fully. Bella wouldn't either.

Moving to the side of the bed, he slid his fingers over her tousled dark hair. She made a soft sound and curled her head against his hand. His gut clenched at her unconscious movement.

He swallowed over a strange lump in his throat and stroked her cheek. Her eyes fluttered open, her violet eyes immediately staring at him. She sighed softly. "Hi," she said. "Have you already done your workout, taken over a half dozen companies and started a new country this morning?"

He gave a wry chuckle and tousled her hair. "No. I worked out. I just thought I should give you fair warning. Both my brothers and their families are descending on me this afternoon."

She searched his face. "You want me to leave?"

He hadn't considered any other possibility. "They'll ask you a million questions."

"You didn't answer my question," she said.

"I want you to do what you want to do," he said.

She sat up, bringing the covers with her. "Well, that doesn't help me any. I mean it would be nice to know if you want to keep me hidden or you don't want them to know about me."

"I'm okay with them knowing about you," he said, watching her carefully. "You're the one who wanted to keep this secret."

She bit her lip and met his gaze. "Well, I have to admit this sounds even better than having dinner at Cie la Sea and seeing a Hawks game in a box seat."

Surprise and amusement rippled through him. "Oh, really? How's that?"

"Getting to meet your brothers," she said. "And they're both obscenely successful, right?"

He nodded. "I guess you might say so."

"And their wives?"

"Yes. What's your point?"

"I love it that they pushed themselves on you this way." She clapped her hands. "I can't imagine you allowing yourself to be pushed by anyone."

"You imagine correctly. I wouldn't let anyone but my brothers get away with this. But we missed too many years together to say no."

She took his hand and held it in hers, her gaze holding his with an emotion that made him feel less empty, less hollow. Damn if he knew why. "I'm in."

Michael sent his limo to pick up his family from the airport. Bella paced the den, checked the mirror a few times to make sure she looked okay. She smoothed her hands over her slacks for the third time and paced again.

"Are you sure you want to meet them?" Michael asked as he glanced up from his laptop.

"Sure, I'm sure," she said, fighting her nerves. "I'm just not sure what to expect or what they'll think of me."

"They'll let me know," Michael said and turned back to his laptop.

"That's great," she said. "So they'll talk about me behind my back."

"Relax. They'll like you," he said.

"How can you be sure?"

"Because your presence will give them something to annoy me about."

She put her hands on her hips. "Why is that?"

"I haven't introduced a lot of women to them," he said, still looking at his screen.

"Why not?"

He shrugged. "I don't know. Just haven't felt like it."

The knowledge gave her a start and she crossed her arms over her chest. "I just hope they're not expecting a super wealthy, sophisticated type—"

"They're not expecting anything because I haven't told them about you."

She felt a stinging pinch to her ego and rolled her eyes at herself. Unable to stand her anxiety any longer, she gave a sigh and turned to leave the room.

"Where are you going?" he called after her.

"To bake a cake," she said.

"Why? That's why I have staff," he said.

"It will give me something to do and make the house smell welcoming," she muttered and continued into the kitchen where the cook was preparing lasagna. "Would I be in your way if I baked a cake?" she asked Gary.

He looked at her in surprise. "Not at all, but I can do it for you."

"I know you can and you could probably do a better job, but I'd like to do it if you don't mind."

Gary's face softened. "Of course. Let me know if I can help you. Do you need a cookbook?"

"No. I've got this one memorized," she said and mixed together one of her favorite cakes from childhood.

Minutes after she put the cake in the oven, the doorbell rang. Her stomach twisted. She heard a chorus of voices, male and female, along with that of a child. She considered hiding in the kitchen, but forced herself into the hallway.

At first glance, she almost couldn't believe how similar the brothers looked. All were tall with dark complexions. One of the brothers had a scar on his cheek, his bone structure somewhat angular. If she hadn't seen him smile, she would have thought he looked like a handsome version of Satan. That one must be Damien.

The other brother held a boy in his arms and a glowing woman stood beside him. From what Michael had told her, she concluded this was Rafe, the playboy brother who'd been tamed by his wife.

Suddenly, she felt Damien's gaze on her. Curiosity glinted in his eyes. "Who do we have here?" he asked Michael.

Michael met her gaze and smiled. "This is Bella St. Clair. Bella, this is my brother Damien and his wife Emma. Rafe, his wife Nicole and his son—"

"Joel," she said, smiling at the adorable boy who looked like a miniature of his father with the exception of his blue eyes.

Rafe lifted his eyebrows. "She has an advantage. She knows more about us than we know about her."

"From what I've heard about the Medici brothers, I need every advantage I can find," she said. "Nice to meet you all."

"Nice to meet you, too," Nicole said, stepping forward. "You're a brave woman facing all of them at once." She paused and sniffed the air. "What is that delicious smell?"

"Michael's cook is preparing lasagna," Bella said.

Nicole shook her head. "No. This is a chocolate smell."

Bella smiled. "Oh, I baked a chocolate cake. It's a favorite recipe from childhood. Chocolate applesauce cake."

"You've just gotten a best friend forever," Rafe said. "My wife is having chocolate cravings that grow more intense each day. I'm having a hard time keeping up."

Nicole swatted at him. "He's joking. This isn't related to my pregnancy. I like chocolate anyway."

"So do I," Emma said and extended her hand. "It's nice to meet you. How did you and Michael meet?"

"At one of his restaurants," she said. "I worked there, but I didn't know he was the owner," she quickly added. "Snowy night, lots of conversation, some surprising things in common."

"Sounds romantic," Emma said.

"It was definitely interesting. I haven't met anyone like him," she said, catching him watching her from the small space that separated them.

"I'm so glad Michael has a...um—" Nicole stopped and laughed. "A friend. He's such a workaholic. Of course, Damien was the same. So was Rafe. He just projected another image, so everyone would think he was a playboy."

"Why are you talking about me as if I'm not here?" Rafe asked.

Gary appeared in the foyer. "I can serve dinner anytime you like."

"Now sounds good," Damien said.

"Big brother has spoken," Michael said good-naturedly. "Five or ten minutes okay?" he asked Gary.

"No problem," Gary said. "The table is waiting."

"I need to go to the bathroom," Joel said.

"I can take him," Nicole said.

"I've got it," Rafe said. "Just point me in the direction of the closest bathroom."

"Down the hall to the left," Bella said.

Nicole watched after Rafe as he led his son down the hallway. "It's hard to believe how quickly he has adapted to being a great father."

"You shouldn't be surprised," Damien said. "The Medici men are overachievers in every area."

Emma leaned her head against his shoulder. "So true. I'm sure you've noticed that about Michael," she said to Bella.

"Fishing, fishing," Michael said under his breath as he slid his hand behind Bella's back and led her into the den. "Forgive my lovely sister-in-law. She may look sweet and demure, but she slayed the dragon known as Damien. Does anyone else want to wash up? There are three more bathrooms on this floor."

Moments later, the group took their seats at Michael's beautiful antique dining room table. Gary served the meal while Michael and his brothers caught up on their business activities.

Afterward, Gary served her cake for dessert.

"Delicious," Emma said. "You must give me your recipe."

"Me, too," Nicole said.

"So, you found a woman who can cook," Rafe said.

"It's news to me," Michael said, meeting Bella's gaze. "But I shouldn't be surprised. She's a multi-talented woman."

"She worked for a charitable organization overseas for a year, is a licensed esthetician, and—"

Embarrassed by the attention, Bella stood and interrupted. "Does anyone want anything else?"

"More cake," Joel said, his face covered in chocolate.

Nicole laughed. "Maybe tomorrow. Bedtime, now."

"Mom," he protested.

"May I read him a bedtime story?" Emma asked.

"I'm sure he would love that," Nicole said then glanced at Bella. "Would you like to join us?"

"Sure, thank you," Bella said and watched as Nicole and Emma cuddled Joel. Emma read a story, then Bella read another before the boy fell asleep.

"Only a two-story night. He must have been tired from all the excitement," Nicole whispered as they left the room.

"Between Damien and Rafe playing with him, I'm surprised he didn't fall asleep during the meal," Emma said.

"Joel was very well-behaved during dinner for being so tired," Bella said. "Would the two of you like to go to the den or the keeping room?"

"Keeping room?" Emma echoed. "What's that?"

"A cozy little room off the kitchen with a fireplace. I suspect the men have taken over the den and are watching a game," Nicole said. "I vote for the keeping room. I noticed Damien really seemed to enjoy Joel. Rafe wondered if the two of you are getting interested in having a child of your own."

"He used to say *never*, then he progressed to maybe. Lately he says *later*." Emma smiled as Bella led the two women toward the kitchen. "I'm perfectly happy taking our time. I'm happier than I ever dreamed possible with Damien." She turned to Bella and sank into an upholstered chair. "What about Michael? How does he feel about children?"

Bella blinked. "Children?" She shook her head. "I wouldn't know. We haven't discussed them, but I know he's happy to be an uncle."

Nicole nodded. "How is Michael doing, really?" she asked. "Rafe has been concerned about him."

"So has Damien," Emma said.

"Really," Bella said, surprise racing through her. "His businesses are doing well and in terms of his health, he works out every morning."

"Yes, but—" Nicole hesitated and sighed. "He's really struggling with the investigation about Leo."

Bella nodded, but she wasn't sure what Nicole was talking about.

"Damien says the latest news from the private investigator really shook him up," Emma said.

What news? Bella wanted to ask, but felt foolish for not knowing. "Michael is a strong man," she said. "I can't imagine anything defeating him."

"I just hate that he continues to torture himself about this. I almost wonder if it would be easier if Leo were pronounced—"

"Don't say that," Nicole said. "Rafe suffers, too. And now knowing that Leo survived the train crash and could have been raised by an abusive man—" Nicole shuddered. "I pray every night that he will be found whole and healthy."

"And ready to reunite with his brothers," Emma said.

"Exactly," Nicole agreed. Silence hovered over the women for a long moment. "I'm glad Michael is doing well. From the way he looks at you, I'm sure you're part of the reason."

Bella wasn't at all sure of that. "Hmm. Would either of you like something to drink? Coffee? Tea?"

"I'd love some hot tea," Emma said.

Bella rose. "Let me get it for you," she murmured and went into the kitchen. Her stomach twisted with agitation as she put the water on and pulled some packets of tea from the cupboard. Why hadn't Michael discussed something so important to him with her? The logical side of her brain immediately came to his defense.

They were having an affair where he dictated the rules. He was completely within his rights to keep the matter about his missing brother private.

After the way he'd insisted that she reveal her painful story about Stephen, though, it didn't seem fair at all. Bella felt like a fool. Why hadn't he told her about the latest developments in the search for Leo? Perhaps because she wasn't truly important.

The knowledge stung. It shouldn't, but it did. She pulled two cups and saucers from the cabinet.

"I can take care of this," Gary said.

She shook her head. "No. I've got it. It's just tea."

"I insist," Gary said, pulling out a tray and cream from the refrigerator. "It is my job."

Stepping back, she smiled although she was still distracted. "Thanks. It's for the two women in the keeping room. I'm going to step out for a breath of fresh air. I'll be back in just a moment."

Bella scooted out the back door and took a deep breath of the chilly winter air. Closing her eyes, she tried to clear her head. She felt hurt and offended. She took another deep breath and wrapped her arms around her waist.

"Too many Medicis for you?" Michael asked, sliding his arm around her back. "Can't say I didn't warn you."

Wondering when he'd joined her, she glanced up at him. "You did warn me."

"Did someone offend you?"

"Hmm," she said and swallowed a wry chuckle. "I guess if anyone offended me, it was me."

His body stiffened. "You? How?"

"It's more about what happened before your family even arrived," she said.

"Is the guessing game necessary or do you want to tell me what this is about?"

"I could say the same about guessing games," she said. "Why didn't you tell me the latest news about Leonardo?"

His face immediately turned dark. "What about Leonardo?"

"The fact that he survived the train crash," she said. "You found that out the night you were sitting in the dark by the fire, didn't you?"

"Yes, I did," he said and moved away from her. "You need to understand that there are some subjects that are off limits."

"To me," she said, angry at herself because this just underscored the fact that she was temporary.

His expression closed up as tight as Fort Knox. "I won't allow this subject to contaminate my time with you. That's my final word."

Eleven

That night was the first time she shared a bed with Michael and they didn't make love. She lay staring up at the ceiling, torn between anger at herself and him. Why should he be the one to call the shots?

Because he was financing her aunt's business.

It seemed, however, that he'd changed the rules when he'd said he wanted her to come to him. Add in the meeting with his family and she didn't know what was going on.

"You're a complicated, difficult man," she said because she knew he was still awake.

"I'm neither," he said. "I'm ordinary."

She laughed. "That's the most ridiculous thing you've ever said."

"I am," he insisted. "I have basic needs. Food, water, sex."

She rolled her eyes. "Along with control, wealth, and a few other things you probably don't realize."

He rolled over and pulled her against him. "Such as?"

She wanted to say *love,* but she wouldn't. "Compassion, affection, understanding."

He shrugged, but slid his fingers through her hair. "Like I said before, there's a difference between need and want."

"So, maybe you want those things," she said, feeling herself sink under the spell of his dark eyes. "There are other things you want, but you'd never admit it."

"Never is a long time," he told her and pulled her on top of him.

Her quarrel with him grew less important with his hard body beneath hers. "Well, it's difficult for me to imagine…"

Sliding his hand behind the nape of her neck, he pulled her mouth against his. "No need to imagine," he said. "I'm here now and so are you."

He seduced her with his sure, magic hands and seductive velvet voice, making her forget her reservations, making her forget that she wanted more than his passion and his body. He took her up and over the top, again and again, and somewhere in that dark night, something changed in her heart….

The next morning, Gary prepared a splendid breakfast and the Medicis enjoyed a rare sunny morning in a private neighborhood park. The three Medici men played ball with Joel, carrying the little boy like a football and making him laugh until he was weak.

Michael lifted his nephew onto his shoulders and carried him around so he could be taller than anyone else.

"That's good father material," Nicole hinted broadly.

The comment made her stomach feel as if she were going up on the down elevator. "I'm sure he'll be a great father when he's ready," Bella said, then tried to change the subject. "When did you say your due date is?"

Soon enough, Rafe checked his watch and announced that it was time to leave. "This has been fun, but some of us have to work tomorrow," he announced.

"And I need a round of pool with Rafe," Damien said. "He's been impossible since I let him beat me."

"Let me?" Rafe said. "You wish."

"We'll see," Damien said.

"Sounds like a challenge to me," Michael said with a secret smile.

"If you came down to South Beach, you could put yourself in the running."

"I'm busy with more important things than billiards at the moment."

"Afraid of getting beat?" Rafe asked.

"You can't goad me," Michael said. "I really do have better things to do."

"Damn." Rafe turned serious. "Are you talking about Leo? You shouldn't let this eat at you so much."

Bella's heart stopped and she stared at Michael.

Michael's gaze turned hard. "I can handle it."

Rafe lifted his brow and shook his head. "Okay." He glanced at Bella. "It was nice meeting you, Bella. Good luck dealing with my brother. He can be ornery as hell, but underneath, way underneath, he's a good guy."

The next day, Michael arrived home at dinnertime. Bella was working late, so he went through the mail. When he saw a package from Italy, his gut clenched.

Curious if this was from his mysterious Aunt Emilia, he quickly opened it. Photographs spilled out.

He held them up and was taken back in time to his childhood. He saw the four wide-eyed faces of him and his brothers dressed in their Sunday best. His gaze wandered to Leo's face and he felt the sting of loss. He wondered how long a person could mourn. Forever, it seemed.

He looked at another photo of a baby held in his father's arms like a football while a toddler craned to see the infant. He turned the photo over and saw a notation scrawled on it. *Baby Michael with brother Leonardo.*

Less than a year younger than Leo, he'd tormented his brother by following him everywhere. He'd been so excited to join his father to ride the train to the baseball game. It would have been his first. He'd even rubbed it in a little to Leo because Leo wanted to go so badly. But Leo had already attended a game with Dad, so it was Michael's turn to go. Until he'd raided the cookie jar before dinner and his parents had decided his discipline would be not going to the game.

To this day, he couldn't eat a cookie without feeling sick to his stomach. His father had died in the train crash and his brother had been missing forever.

His stomach twisting with a guilt that wouldn't pass, he found a short note behind the photos. *Dear Michael, I wanted you to have these photographs your father sent me so many years ago. I am so glad that you and your brothers have found each other and are keeping your family bond alive. Do not ever give up on each other. Love Emilia.*

Michael stared at the note and photos, fighting a

warring combination of sweet memories and nauseat-
ing loss. A day didn't pass when he failed to think of
Leo, but seeing this underscored his need for resolution.

Unwilling to discuss this with his brothers, Michael
called his investigator. "Have you made any progress?" he asked, not bothering to keep the impatience
from his voice.

"These things take time," the investigator said.

"You've been saying that for months," Michael said.

"Look, I believe your brother may have survived the
crash. I believe he was taken in by a woman who
couldn't have children."

"Names, what are their names?"

"She went by a different name than her husband, and
apparently her husband went by several different names."

Michael frowned. "Several names. He must've been
a criminal."

"Some records indicate he'd been charged with
petty theft. When I checked three of the names, I got
a bunch of complaints about grifting. Some that involved a boy."

Michael closed his eyes. "What was the boy's
name?"

"Depends," Carson said. "John, George, but no Leo.
The complaints that included a mention of the boy stopped
when your brother would have been about fifteen."

"Do you think he died?" he asked. "Or was killed?"

"Either of those could have happened, but there's
another possibility. He could have disappeared and
changed his identity."

"I want a written report of everything you've found.
Is the woman who kept him still alive?"

"No, and I'm not too sure about the man, either. I'm

still working that end of the lead, but I have to pursue others, too."

"Okay," Michael said with a sigh. "Keep me posted."

The rainy day matched Bella's mood. Since it was slow that morning at the spa, she urged Charlotte to get out and take a break while Bella manned the reception desk. It took some arm-twisting, but Charlotte finally agreed.

With no customers in sight, Bella sipped a latte as she tried to distract herself by reading the paper. She was still angry with herself for expecting Michael to share more of himself with her. When he'd decided to introduce her to his family, she'd let her guard down. She should remember that he viewed her as temporary and she should always, always do the same.

Under the downtown community section, a short article caught her eye. The article reported how a fire had destroyed a community center, the same one where she and Michael had worked that Saturday. An anonymous donor had stepped up to pay for a new center to be built.

Her heart skipped over itself and suspicion raced through her. A warm, lovely kind of suspicion. Anonymous donor. She'd just bet she knew who that was.

Bella sighed. How was she supposed to tell herself that she shouldn't care about Michael when he did these kinds of things? Just when she thought he was too hard and remote, he did something to turn her opinion of him upside down.

Michael heard the side door open. "Hello?" Bella called. "Anybody home? Anybody want a hot dog with mustard and chili and greasy French fries just because it's Monday and it's raining?"

She walked into the den still wearing a yellow slicker and carting a paper bag and what he would guess were two milk shakes.

He chuckled. "Sounds good. Gary may not like it, though. He thinks you're going to put him out of a job."

She shook her head. "Ridiculous. I can make a few things, but he's the professional. Where do you want to eat?"

"In here," he said. "What kind of milk shake did you get me?"

She tossed him a sideways glance. "How do you know I got one for you? I may have gotten both of them for me."

He grinned. "I guess I'll just have to see if I can negotiate one from you."

"It's possible," she said, pulling off her jacket. "I hope you like chocolate."

"I do," he said. She made the room brighter, somehow.

"Okay, then, if you answer this question honestly, I will give you a chocolate shake," she said and unpacked the bags, giving him two hot dogs while she took one.

"Depends on the question," he said, joining her at the table.

She nodded. "During one of my breaks today, I was reading the newspaper." She lifted a French fry to his lips and he ate it.

"And?"

"Well, you remember that community center we were painting, the one that blew up?"

"Yes," he said and took a bite out of one of the hot dogs. "This is really good."

She shot him a conspiratorial smile. "I agree. Back to the newspaper. There was an article about how the community center is going to be torn down and a new one is going to be built in its place."

"That's good," he said, continuing to eat his meal.

"An anonymous donor has made this possible," she said, regarding him with deep suspicion. "You wouldn't happen to know anything about this donor, would you?"

"I suspect if the donor is anonymous then he—" He swallowed another bite. "Or she prefers to remain anonymous."

She slumped. "You're not going to tell me, are you?"

"Tell you what?"

"If you are the anonymous donor," she said.

"Me?" he asked, injecting shock into his voice. "Why would I part with my money to fund a community center that could very well end up doing an inefficient job helping the children who need the services?"

She looked away. "True. You're not the type to have a soft spot for a cause, especially after you've suffered burns from rescuing a child at the community center."

"Right," he said.

"Rescuing a child like that wouldn't have an impact on you. You wouldn't be concerned about that child's future in a community center."

"The old building was a fire hazard," he said.

"A terrible one," she agreed.

"They'd damn well better make sure the new one isn't," he muttered.

Bella looked at him and held his gaze for a moment then slid the milk shake to him.

"I didn't tell you who the anonymous donor was," he said.

"That's okay. I have an idea of my own. Want me to describe him?"

He shrugged. "If you want."

"He's hot," she said.

"Oh, really?" he said, lifting his brow at her.

She nodded. "He's the kind who pretends he doesn't care."

"Pretends?"

She nodded again. "He's all about the bottom line."

"What other line is there?"

She leaned toward him and took his chin in her hand in a surprisingly aggressive move that he liked. "You're such a faker," she whispered and kissed him.

The more time he spent with Bella, the more he wanted her. This wasn't going the way he'd planned. He'd expected to get his fill of her then both of them would move on. The next two evenings, he even came home early so he could spend more time with her.

In the morning, he rose early as he always did and exercised in his gym. When he returned to his bedroom, he found her reading from a folder.

She quickly set the folder down beside her and smiled. "How was the elliptical?"

"You're awake. What were you reading?" he asked, but he already knew. He took a quick, sharp breath to control his anger.

She cleared her throat. "Um, it was on the nightstand. I knocked it off when I went to the bathroom."

"You didn't notice the label said Leo," he said, clenching his teeth.

She seemed to catch on that he was displeased. She

bit her lip and looked away. "I'm sorry. I know this is important to you and you won't discuss it with me. It's hard for me to feel shut out on this. I want to help you."

"You can't," he said. "It's a matter of patient, resilient research by a knowledgeable investigator. I'm going in the shower. If you want to read it while I'm in the shower, go ahead. When I get out, I'll be putting the report away and we won't discuss it."

"But," she began.

"This is nonnegotiable, Bella. Don't push it," he said and went into the bathroom to try to wash the guilt about his brother from his skin, from inside him. He knew, however, that it wouldn't work. He also knew that he couldn't, wouldn't discuss Leo with Bella. Her empathy would be harder to bear than his own self-condemnation.

"You're late," Charlotte said as Bella returned from her lunch on Saturday. "I can't keep up with you. One week you're working overtime. The next week you're spacey and late."

"I'm sorry," Bella said, pulling on the jacket that bore the name of her aunt's business. "I have a lot on my mind."

"Does his name start with M?" Charlotte asked. "What's going on between you two?"

"It's complicated," Bella said. Her heart and mind were still reeling after reading the P.I.'s report. It hit her again that all the Medici brothers had suffered terribly. Knowing how much Michael still grieved brought tears to her eyes. She took a deep breath. "There's more to him than meets the eye."

"That can be good."

"I can't talk about it yet. He would be furious," Bella said. "Just trust me that I want to help him. I need to help him."

Charlotte frowned. "It's nothing illegal, is it?"

Bella shook her head. "Nothing illegal."

Charlotte shrugged. "Okay, just try not to be late. Your client is waiting for you to work your magic. Can you close up tonight? Fred is taking me out for lobster."

"Hmm," Bella said with a smile. "Looks like you and Fred are turning into a regular thing."

Charlotte scowled at her. "Get to work."

Bella worked nonstop until 6:00 p.m., but the entire time she was thinking about Michael and his brother Leo. If Michael was able to answer his questions about Leo, she wondered if Michael would finally be at peace. She wondered what kind of person he would be. She wondered if he would be free to love and be loved.

Despite all his success and hard work, Michael felt unworthy of love. She identified it because she had felt that way after her mother had abandoned her. After all, if her own mother had dumped her, wouldn't everyone else?

Stephen had made her believe in the possibility of love. She thought he'd believed in her. She'd thought he'd been committed. She was the one who'd left to pursue her dream and left her aunt and Stephen behind. Even though Stephen had encouraged her, he'd needed her when he'd lost his job and his confidence. She'd thought Stephen was the sweetest man in the world. Lately, she wasn't as sure about Stephen as she once had been. He just didn't seem as sincere.

She was sure that although Michael was as sincere as the day was long, he also was not the sweetest man in the world. His background had given him rough edges. He didn't love her. He wanted her. The more she was with him, the more she wanted him freed from his demons. Without those demons, he would be so much happier, so much more fulfilled. Free to love and receive the love he deserved, even if she wasn't the one for him.

Twelve

Bella whisked into Michael's home a bit later than she'd planned on Monday. "Hello? Any news?"

Silence followed. "I'm in the den."

Bella felt a sinking sensation in her stomach and rushed to the den. "Is there a problem?"

"No." His gaze was shuttered. "Why do you ask?"

"Because you sound like someone has pushed your mute button," she said.

One side of his lips lifted in amusement. "I'm fine. No hot dogs?"

"No. I was slammed at work then had to run errands. I can fix some if you like," she offered.

"No. Gary can prepare something for us."

"I always feel guilty about that," she said. "We're just two people. We should be able to fix our own."

"I can afford it," he said.

"Still," she said.

"What do you want for dinner?"

"I'll fix a peanut butter and honey sandwich with bananas and potato chips," she said adamantly.

He chuckled. "He's planning shrimp creole for me."

"Oh, that sounds delicious," she said, her mouth watering.

"Wouldn't want to keep you from your peanut butter sandwich."

"You're an evil man," she said.

His face hardened. "You're not the first to know that."

The self-contempt in his gaze took her breath away. "Michael, you have to tell me what happened. Something happened."

"Another dead lead," he said and shrugged. "Nothing new."

"I've been thinking about this," she said eagerly.

"Thinking about what?" he asked, his gaze cold.

"Thinking about Leo," she said. "After I read the investigator's report, I wondered if you should put an ad in some of the Pennsylvania newspapers."

"If that were the best way to proceed, the investigator would suggest it," he said.

"But what if you and your brothers did it?" she asked. "Maybe that would have more impact than it would from the P.I."

Michael's nostrils flared in anger as he looked at her. "Bella, we've already discussed this. It's none of your business."

"But you're suffering," she said, clenching her fists. "I can't stand it."

He lifted his hand. "Enough. I'm spending the night alone. You're on your own."

She felt as if he'd stabbed her by shutting her out. "Michael," she said.

"Good night," he said and turned away.

Frustrated and hurt, Bella wanted to throw something against the floor-to-ceiling windows and make them break. She wanted to break down this barrier between her and Michael. Their relationship had become very different from what it had been when it started. Every now and then she felt as if she were getting past the walls Michael had built around himself, but then she felt as if the walls were forged from concrete.

"Oh," she groaned, pushing her hair from her face. Why should she stay here? She would just become more frustrated and upset. Fine, he said she was on her own. She would leave.

The following day, Bella inwardly fumed, practicing a half dozen speeches designed to set Michael straight, as if such a thing were possible. As if he'd listen to her for more than three seconds. Not on the subject of Leo. After lunch, she was still in flux about her evening plans. If her aunt weren't so busy with her new beau, Bella would have spent the evening with her.

"Bella," Charlotte called in a singsong voice. "You have a visitor."

Bella glanced up to see Michael standing next to the front desk. Surprise washed over her, although she was still peeved with him.

"Don't worry about a thing. I've looked at the book, and Donna and I can take all your appointments. It won't be any trouble at all," Charlotte said.

"Take my appointments," she echoed, confused. "Why?"

Charlotte smiled coyly. "I'll let Michael tell you. But don't worry about your other appointments today. I've got those handled, too."

"What?" she asked as Charlotte walked away. "What is she talking about?"

"I'm considering buying a property in Grand Cayman," Michael said.

"That's nice," she said, looking away from his gaze, wanting to hang on to her anger. Her anger would keep her safe from getting more emotionally intertwined with him.

"I'm flying down there this afternoon and coming back on Saturday morning."

She shrugged. "Have a nice trip."

"I want you to join me," he said.

She blinked and met his gaze. "This afternoon?" She shouldn't go. Who did he think he was telling her to join him with zero notice? *Join him for a trip to a luxurious Caribbean island where it was warm instead of gray and gloomy.* "I can't imagine leaving Charlotte in the lurch like this, especially on Saturday."

"I discussed it with Charlotte and she's all for it."

"I don't want Charlotte overworking," she said, fidgeting as visions of her and Michael walking along a beautiful beach danced in her head.

"Has she been overworking?" he asked.

"Well, no, not yet, but—" She broke off, feeling pinned by his gaze.

"Are you afraid of going with me?"

Her stomach dipped. "Of course not. Why would I be afraid?" Because she was starting to develop feelings for him, strong feelings that could cause problems for her later.

"You tell me," he said.

When she didn't answer, he shrugged his broad shoulders. "I won't force you to go. If you're not interested in stepping into water so clear you can see down fifty feet and—"

"Okay, okay," she said and told him the same thing she had when his brothers had come to town. "I'm in."

"Fine," he said. "We can leave from here. I'll buy everything you'll need down there."

"But can't I pick up just a few things? I don't want to spend my time there shopping."

He gave a wry chuckle. "Not something I would expect to hear from a woman. You don't want to spend your time shopping. Okay. I'll have the driver stop by your apartment. You have one hour."

"Sheesh. "Do you ever give a girl some notice?" she muttered. "Aunt Charlotte, I'm headed out," she called.

Charlotte beamed and walked over to give her a hug. "Take pictures."

"Camera," Bella said, imprinting the item on her list. "Must bring camera."

"And have a good time."

"Are you sure you'll be okay?" Bella asked, suddenly worried again.

"I'll be fine. You shouldn't pass this up." She glanced at Michael. "Treat her right or you'll find a pair of scissors in your head when you least expect it."

"Whoa," he said and gave her a mock salute. "I'll make sure she has a good time."

"You do that," Charlotte said then clapped her hands. "Now get going. Daylight's burning!"

Four hours later, they were sitting at a restaurant on the ocean watching the sunset as they were served a gourmet meal. A parrot squawked in the background and a warm breeze slid over her skin.

"Uncle," she said.

"Uncle what?" Michael asked.

"I can't deny that this is incredible. The food, the sunset, everything."

"It's not bad, is it?" he said. "Grand Cayman is one of the more civilized islands. Rarely gets hit by hurricanes, but it can happen. The rainy season is supposed to be unpleasant. You'll have to tell me what you think after you've spent more time here."

"I can tell you already that it's a wonderful break from winter, if that's what you're looking for," she said.

"That," he said. "And I always consider the investment benefit. This would be more for fun, though."

She smiled at him. "Oh, my. I thought you weren't interested in spending money for fun."

He slid her a sideways glance. "I can do fun things. I just haven't been motivated until recently."

"And why is that?" she asked, lifting her glass of wine to her lips and taking a sip.

"I think you know it's because of you," he said.

"Hard for me to believe I have any influence over you." She stared out at the ocean, drinking in the sight.

"Is that what you want? Influence over me?" he asked.

She met his gaze. "I want you to be happy."

Something flashed in his eyes, something she couldn't identify at first glance because it came and went so quickly. "And you think you know what would make me happy."

"That sounds potentially arrogant, but I think I have an idea of what might help. Not that I'll get a chance to help with that."

"Why do you care about my happiness?" he asked. "You're getting what you want. I've funded your aunt's business. You know I'm not going to renege."

Her stomach twisted and she frowned. "I don't know. Maybe I'm more of a sap than I thought I was." She met his gaze again. "Or maybe there's more to you than I thought there was."

"That last one would be wrong. I'm shallow," he insisted.

"Yes," she said. "That's why you agreed to resuscitate my aunt's business."

"I benefit from that agreement in several ways."

"It was still coloring outside your lines. You're a liar if you disagree," she said.

His eyes lit with amusement, but he said nothing.

"And there's the matter of the community center," she said.

"Anonymous could be anyone."

"Uh-huh," she said. "There's another subject that reveals your tender side, but you get all touchy when I bring it up, so I won't."

"Thank you," he said and nodded toward the horizon. "Don't miss the sunset."

She watched the orange ball sink lower and a green light followed it. "I've never seen that before," she said. "What was it?"

"A green flash," he said. "I'm not much for legends, but legend has it that seeing it means you have the ability to see into another person's heart."

"So, you don't believe it," she said.

He paused. "I didn't say that."

She leaned toward him. "You could have any woman. Why do you want me?"

He shook his head. "Too many reasons. Would you like dessert?"

She also shook her head. "No. I'm ready to go if you are."

Minutes later, the driver drove them down a winding road to a gated driveway which opened after the driver punched in a code. It was a clear night, and the moonlight glowed on the stucco mansion with colored roof tiles as they drove toward it.

Bella sucked in her breath at the beauty of the building and the lush green foliage. She looked at Michael. "I must have misunderstood. I thought you were looking at a condominium."

"The condo's on Seven Mile beach. This one would be for personal use." The driver pulled to a stop and they got out.

Bella looked up at the size of the mansion. "It's lovely from the outside."

"Let's take a look inside," he said and unlocked the front door. Cool marble floors and upscale island decor greeted them.

"Very nice," she said.

He took her hand in his and wandered through the house. All the modern necessities and wants anyone could imagine were included in the home along with several views designed to make a mere mortal drool, even at night.

They stood on a deck for a moment and Bella drank in the gentle sound of the ocean against the sand. "Oh, I think we'd better leave right away," she said.

"Why?"

"Because I don't know how anyone could leave after staying here five minutes," she said.

He laughed and tugged her hand. "Let's go upstairs."

Reluctantly leaving the deck, she climbed the stairs and looked at the hallways of bedrooms, another deck and finally the master suite. She followed him inside, glancing up to see the stars in the skylights which featured blinds for closing. A floor-to-ceiling window which revealed a fantastic view of the sea and the sky sat opposite the large bed. She walked through the sliding-glass door on to yet another deck with an awning, chairs and table and Jacuzzi.

"Ohhhh, this is so good it's bad," she said.

"You like it?" he asked, pulling her against him as he looked out at the ocean.

"Who wouldn't?" she asked, looking up at him.

"Relaxing has never been my forte," he said. "I've received solicitations like this before, but I ignored them. Who has time for trips to the Cayman Islands?"

She saw a lostness in his eyes and her stomach twisted. "Has it ever occurred to you to take a vacation?"

"I've taken vacations. Mountain climbing, scuba diving…"

"No, I mean a real vacation where you actually relax," she said. "Maybe even, heaven forbid, sleep late and ditch your workout for one whole day."

His lips twitched. "Not really."

"Why doesn't that surprise me? I wonder what it would take to get you to sleep late," she said.

His eyes darkened. "Try and find out."

After a night of lovemaking, she felt him stir in the morning. Determined to keep him from getting out of bed, she rolled on top of him, still half-asleep. "Nuh-uh," she said. "You're not going anywhere."

She opened her eyes to find his sleepy eyes staring back at hers. "How are you going to keep me here?"

"One way or another," she said and pressed her mouth against his for a long kiss.

His hands skimmed over her buttocks. "You're cute when you're slee—"

She wiggled lower, sliding on to his hardness, taking the words from his mouth. "Ohhhh," he said.

She began to ride, forcing her eyes to open so she could see the ecstasy on his face. He wrapped his hands about her hips again, guiding her, distracting her. She was supposed to be in control, but he took it from her.

Soon, her pleasure splintered from her and she squeezed him tight within her. His gasps of pleasure fed hers and she climaxed just as the sun peeked through the horizon.

Seconds, minutes, hours later, Michael slid his leg over her. "Lord, woman, what time is it?"

"I don't know and I don't care," she said.

He chuckled, nuzzling her head. He shifted her slightly then swore. "It's eight-thirty. Do you know the last time I slept this late?"

"Not last weekend," she said.

"That's true," he said, rising. "The last time I slept this late, I was thirteen and sick with strep throat."

She waved her hand upward and he caught it. "What do you want?"

"To feel your forehead to make sure you don't have strep throat," she said.

He chuckled and lifted her hand to his mouth instead. "No strep throat. What do you want for breakfast? There's staff downstairs waiting for our order."

She sighed. "Sometimes, I want no staff," she said. "I'm good with a bagel."

"We'll do that next visit. What do you want this time?"

"Scrambled eggs, blueberry pancakes and crisp bacon," she said.

"That's a little more than a bagel," he said.

"Yeah, well if they're dying to fix breakfast…" she said and suddenly felt guilty. "Scratch that," she said. "I'm okay with toast."

"Liar," he said. "Bella wants pancakes. Bella will have pancakes."

Crap, she thought. She'd better not get used to this.

After breakfast, she and Michael explored the house then changed into swimsuits to sun on the private beach. Michael wasn't the type to sit still, so he read for a while then dragged her into the water.

She stared at her feet next to his, marveling at how clear the water was. Tiny fishes swam between their legs. "Omigosh, this is amazing."

"Look farther out," he said, pointing to where the water was deeper.

She spotted larger, multicolored fish and a dolphin jumping. "It's so calm and clear you don't even need to snorkel."

"One of the reasons I like it here," he said.

"How often have you been?" she asked.

"Just a couple times. Always business," he said. He tugged her deeper into the water and dunked her.

She gasped as she returned to the surface. "Why did you do that?" she asked, swatting at his muscular chest. She may as well have been a fly.

"You looked like you needed to get wet all over," he said, grinning as he pulled her against him.

"How about a warning next time?" she demanded, wrapping her legs around his waist because it seemed like the natural thing to do.

He shook his head, his dark eyes glinting in the sun like black diamonds. "Too much fun taking you by surprise," he said and took her mouth before she could protest.

With the water and Michael's arms surrounding her, she felt herself sinking under his spell. What a magical moment to be with him. Away from everything but each other.

Seconds later, she felt her bathing-suit top slip from her body. "What—"

Michael grinned like a demon and moved away from her.

"You," she accused, going after him, but he was faster. "Michael," she called. "Give me back my swimsuit."

"In a while," he said. "Since we have a private beach, you can go topless."

"Some other time," she said, swimming toward him.

"I dare you," he said.

She stopped and groaned. "Oh, don't say that."

"Ah, so you can't turn down a dare, either," he said, reminding her of how she'd challenged him to help paint the community center.

"That was different. You got to keep your clothes on."

"And burn my hands," he said.

"True," she muttered, still reluctant. She met his gaze, for once nearly carefree and she realized she would do just about anything for him to stay that way instead of tortured and mired in guilt.

Taking a deep breath, she closed her eyes. *I can do this,*

she told herself. *I can do this.* She opened her eyes and walked forward, biting her lip as her upper body broke the surface of the water. Even though Michael had seen her naked too many times to count, this just felt different.

She couldn't quite meet his gaze. "Never let it be said—"

He swooped her into his arms, his chest covering hers as he carried her into deeper water. "I really didn't think you'd do it."

She gawked at him. "You dared me. What am I supposed to do?"

"Remind me to never let you around any other men who like to make dares," he said gruffly.

She looked at him. "I'm selective," she said.

"Keep it that way," he said.

Thirteen

They returned to Atlanta on Saturday in time for Bella to attend the wedding of a college friend. The trip to Grand Cayman had been amazing. She'd never seen Michael in a fun mode before. It lifted her heart and made her want to see more of that from him.

As they returned home, however, she saw him pulling into himself more and more. They parted ways at the private airport. He tucked her into his limo and she returned to her apartment.

Dressing for the wedding, Bella couldn't help wondering about her own future. What did Michael want from her? She couldn't believe he wanted marriage, yet she knew he didn't want her to be involved with any other man.

She drove to the church where her old friend CeCe was married then went to a country club for the reception. She smiled as CeCe danced first with her new husband and then her father. A bite of nostalgia prodded her at the memory of her own father, whom she'd never known, and her mother, who had died.

"They look happy," a male voice said from behind her.

She turned at the sound of Stephen's voice and nodded. "They do." She glanced over her shoulder at him, looking for his fiancée. "Where's your fiancée?"

He met her gaze. "Where's your friend? Michael Medici?"

"We just got back from Grand Cayman. He had some work to do," she said.

"You're traveling in different circles these days," Stephen said. "Michael Medici's pretty high on the food chain."

"You're traveling in different circles now, too," she said. "Excuse me—"

"No," he said, blocking her way. "There's no reason for us to be awkward. You and I have known each other too long. Let me get you a drink."

She took a deep breath and looked at his familiar blond hair and blue eyes and relaxed. This was Stephen. She'd known him a long time. He'd been important to her and now he wanted to be her friend. The sting of longing she usually felt for him was absent.

"Okay," she finally said. "White wine," she said.

"I know that," he said with a smile and left to get a drink for her.

Shortly, he returned with a beer for himself and a glass of wine for her. "How did you like Grand Cayman?"

"It was amazing. The water was so clear," she said.

"And Michael, what is he like?"

She tilted her head to the side. "Complex," she said.

"One time I think I've got his personality nailed, then seconds later, I learn more about him."

"Hmm," Stephen said.

"What about your job?" she asked. "Are you liking it?"

"I like being employed," he said and paused. "Britney is a means to an end."

She gasped, shocked at his response. "But you do love her."

He shrugged. "In a way, I guess," he said, lifting his beer and taking a long swallow. "But I've never gotten over you."

Dismayed by his declaration, she shook her head. "I thought you had fallen in love with Britney."

"In a way," he repeated, covering her hand with his. "But you know I've loved you forever, Bella."

"But you broke up with me."

He shrugged again. "I knew Britney could help me get ahead. But you and I had something special. There's no reason we can't continue."

She blinked. "Not if you're engaged, we can't."

"There's no reason you and I can't enjoy each other. After all, you and Michael are enjoying each other."

"What does that have to do with anything?"

"If you and Michael can have an affair, why can't you and I?"

"You are engaged," she said.

"If you're willing to give yourself to Michael, why wouldn't you give yourself to me?" he asked, taking her hand and pressing his mouth against hers.

Bella jerked away, turning her face. She stood, barely holding back the desire to throw her wine in his face. "Again, because you're engaged. Michael is not."

"Bella, you're Michael Medici's mistress," he said. "I can afford you now, too."

"No," she said, nauseated by Stephen's proposal. "Never." She turned around and walked right into Michael's hard chest.

Michael looked at her and Stephen with a scathing glance. Bella opened her mouth to explain, but Michael turned toward Stephen.

"Leave her alone," he said. "You left her behind. She is with me now. If I hear of you bothering her again, your current job could suddenly disappear." He turned to Bella. "Let's go," he said and escorted her from the room to the front door. "How could you let him touch you?"

"I didn't want to. He took me by surprise," she said.

"You must have known he would be here," Michael said, his jaw twitching.

"I didn't," she said. "It's true that Stephen is friends with this couple, too, but I didn't know if he would attend. I was sure his fiancée would be with him if he did." She paused a half beat. "Besides, if I were intent on getting together with Stephen, why would I have invited you to come with me this afternoon?"

"Let's go back to my house," he said and waved for the valet. "I'll take you."

"But my car," she began.

"I'll send a driver for it," he said.

With Stephen's insulting remarks, the event had already been ruined for her, so she was all too happy to leave. The drive was silent, and Michael's brooding disposition made the air in the car so thick she could hardly breathe.

As soon as they arrived at Michael's house, he whisked her up to his bedroom. She hated for him to be upset, but she didn't feel she deserved his wrath. "I realize it may have looked damaging, but you have to believe I didn't invite his advance. You shouldn't be angry at me."

He took a deep breath, his nostrils flaring with emotion. "I'm not angry at you. I'm furious with Stephen. What the hell gave him the idea that he could treat you like that?"

She shook her head, but her stomach sank. "He seemed to have figured out that you and I have an arrangement. This is what I was afraid of, that people would find out that I could be bought."

Michael sliced his hand through the air. "Under the right circumstances, everyone can be bought."

His assessment only made her feel worse. "Actions can be bought, but emotions can't."

"You may have agreed to our affair to help your aunt, but things are different. Can you tell me that the only reason you're with me is because of your aunt?"

The oxygen seemed to disappear from her lungs. "You know I can't," she whispered.

He pulled her against him. "Damn right you can't," he muttered and took her mouth. The passion between them exploded, burning boundaries, excuses and denial. Perhaps a part of her had sensed from the beginning that Michael would change her life. Perhaps the passion they'd shared in the beginning had been a clue and she'd run from it, run from him, because he was a hard, complicated man. How could she ever hope to win his heart? If he even possessed one.

With no holds barred, he stripped off her clothes and his and imprinted his body against hers. He made love to her from head to toe, bringing her to ecstasy again and again. It was as if he wanted to mark her as his woman.

But how could that be possible? He'd always made it clear their relationship was temporary, with no messy emotional ties. She couldn't deny it any longer. She felt a part of him. She craved his happiness, his safety, his well-being in a way she'd never experienced with Stephen.

The knowledge rolled through her like thunder. She loved Michael.

"I want to wipe the thought of every other man from your mind," he muttered against her as his muscular body pumped into her. "I want you to know that you belong to me."

Panting from their wild lovemaking and her own realization, she buried her head against his throat, damp with sweat from his restraint.

"I know," she said. "I know. I love you," she whispered into his ear. "But will you ever belong to me?"

He stiffened and thrust inside her one last time, his climax written on every cell of his body and echoed on his face.

Her heart hammered as they collapsed in each other's arms. Had she really said that? Had she really uttered the three words? Had she asked him if he would be hers? She waited, holding her breath. Maybe he would give her the words she secretly longed to hear. Maybe he would tell her that she had become so important to him that he would never let her go.

Michael stroked her hair. "Go to sleep."

Her chest twisted with disappointment. When had this happened? When had he consumed her? And how was she going to survive knowing he didn't love her?

She fell into a troubled sleep, but awakened when she

felt the absence of his body. He was working out as usual, she thought. Her body craved more sleep, but a part of her craved seeing him more. She glanced at the clock, estimating he was fifteen minutes into his routine.

Dragging herself from the bed, she splashed her face with water and brushed her teeth then wandered down the hall to find him on the elliptical, his back to her. Knowing he still had free weights to go, she waited on the couch in their suite and leaned her head back against the wall.

Michael doubled his workout. He had never felt this way about a woman. He could have easily punched Bella's former lover in the face. Perhaps he should have. Maybe it would have gotten his completely alien possessiveness for Bella out of his system. The woman was having a very odd effect on him. Lord knew, he wasn't the type to take a vacation, let alone *really* enjoy a vacation home, but spending time with Bella without the constant press of work appealed to him. When in hell had that happened?

He didn't know what the solution was. He refused to give her up, but he wasn't sure how to keep her. She was a woman full of passion and heart. He wanted both, but he didn't possess much of the latter, and hadn't for a long time. Giving up his heart had been necessary for survival. If he didn't care, then he wouldn't hurt. If he didn't hope, then he wouldn't be disappointed. Most importantly, if he didn't count on another human being to be with him, then he would know how to stand on his own. Always alone.

He finished his free-weight repetitions and returned to the suite. He spotted Bella asleep, propped on the couch.

His throat tightened with an odd emotion. She looked so sweet and vulnerable.

He bent down beside her and just looked at her for a long moment. Her dark eyelashes fanned out from ivory skin with just a little pink from the Cayman sun left in her cheeks. He felt a stir of pleasure at the memory of how much she'd enjoyed the short trip. He'd already made an offer on the house. He would take her again and other places, too.

"Hey, sleepyhead," he said, touching her soft cheek.

She stirred, looking up at him with sleepy eyes. "Hi," she said in a husky voice.

"Hi to you. What are you doing out of bed? This is no time for angels. This is the time of demons," he said. It had long been the hour he'd chased the demons from his mind.

"I didn't want you to start work without getting to see you," she said, lifting her arms.

Unable to refuse her, he sat on the couch beside her and held her. "I do have work to catch up on, but I won't be in the office all day."

"That's good," she said and looked up at him. "I'm going to visit my aunt today. I feel like I should check up on her to make sure she's okay."

"Any reason to believe otherwise?" he asked.

"No, but she was such a faker when I was overseas, I'm determined to keep tabs on her now."

He chuckled and nodded. "Fool me once, shame on you," he said, quoting the old proverb.

"Fool me twice, shame on me," she finished and sighed as they walked into his bedroom. She looked up at him. "I forgot to thank you for coming to the wedding reception last night."

"I wish I could say it was my pleasure."

"Me, too, but after what Stephen said—"

He pressed his finger to her lips. "Don't think of it again."

She winced. "I can't promise that, but I'll try." Her face turned solemn. "I love you," she said.

His heart stopped. She pronounced it as the sun rose, illuminating the room. Bold and brave, she blew him away. He didn't know how to respond.

She bit her lip. "I thought I knew what love was before. With Stephen."

His stomach twisted and he felt his hands draw into fists, but he held his tongue.

"But I didn't," she said. "I can't remember wanting someone else's happiness more in my life. Ever. I would do anything for you to feel happy and at peace. I love you."

Overwhelmed by her profession, he pulled her against him. Humbled, but unable to offer her the same, he slid his fingers through her lush hair. "You're so sweet," he said. "So precious. I've never met another woman like you." He held her close for several moments where his insides twisted and turned. "You had a rough day and night. You should get more rest," he said. "Go back to bed."

She looked up and met his gaze, and he knew he hadn't given her what she wanted. He knew she wanted more from him. What she didn't realize was that he didn't have it to give.

Bella returned to Michael's bed, but her slumber was filled with strange dreams. When she rose a couple hours later, she was more tired than rejuvenated. She also felt her profession of love sitting between her and

Michael like an undigested Thanksgiving meal. Heavy and uncomfortable.

Well, now she'd gone and done it. She'd blurted out her love to him and he didn't know what to do with it. The awkwardness of that moment hung over her like a guillotine. Why had she done it? Because she couldn't stop herself. A dam had broken open inside her.

With a mixture of humiliation and disappointment, she got herself together and drove to visit her aunt. Bad move. Charlotte's boyfriend, Fred, answered the door.

Charlotte soon followed, wrapped in a long silk robe. "Bella, I didn't know you were planning a visit. Come inside." Her aunt dragged her toward the kitchen.

"That's okay. I don't want to interrupt," Bella said.

"Nonsense, Fred was just going to take a shower." She gave him a quick kiss. "Let me get you some orange juice and blueberry muffins. I want to hear about Grand Cayman," she said, heading for the refrigerator. "Should I go?"

"Yes," Bella said, stunned at the speed of her aunt's developing relationship with Fred. "It's beautiful."

"Even for the not obscenely rich?" Charlotte asked, handing Bella a glass of orange juice and some muffins.

"Yes, even for the middle class. The water is warm and clear and the waves gentle. There's a place that looks like lava where the water spouts. And they have great food. Low crime." She took a sip of orange juice.

"Sounds like heaven. So, has Michael asked you to marry him?"

Bella choked. "No," she managed.

"Why not?" Charlotte demanded.

"What about you and Fred?" she asked, changing the subject.

Charlotte waved her hand. "He has asked, but I'm procrastinating."

"Why?" Bella asked. "Don't you like him?"

"Yes, but marriage… I did that once and it didn't turn out well at all."

"Do you love him?" Bella asked.

Charlotte paused. "I think I might," she admitted. "But if I get sick again?"

Bella covered her aunt's hands with hers. "I hope you won't live your life that way."

Charlotte took a deep breath and shot Bella a sly smile. "And here I thought we were talking about your romance. How did we get off track?"

"We're not," Bella said, forcing a smile. "Michael's not the marrying kind. I'm not sure he even believes in love."

"Oh, sweetie, I'm so sorry," Charlotte said. "And I pushed you into this."

Bella shook her head. "No, you didn't. I went into it on my own. He's from a tough background. I can't really blame him."

Charlotte's eyes filled with tears. "I wanted you to get over Stephen. I knew he wasn't right for you. I had this feeling about Michael. I'm sorry."

Bella shrugged. "Stop it. He's an amazing man. I just don't think he's interested in forever after."

"Are you going to break it off with him?" Charlotte asked.

Bella's mind reeled at the thought. "Oh, wow." She shook her head. "I'm not there yet. We'll see."

Fred returned from the shower. "Any blueberry muffins left for me?"

Bella smiled, but her heart twisted. She couldn't help being happy for her aunt. Charlotte had been through so much, and now she had a man who clearly wanted to be with her regardless of the iffy future.

On the other hand, Michael was a man who didn't believe in love, and Bella feared he never would.

Fourteen

Over the next seven days, Bella waited. She held her breath waiting for a true response from Michael. Something more than him ignoring the love she'd professed to him. But each day and night he said nothing different. He praised her beauty, made love to her, but avoided any real emotional confession.

For Bella, every minute that he ignored her confession she felt her hope grow smaller and smaller. Did her feelings mean so little to him? Did *she* mean so little to him?

On the eighth day, she gave it another shot. They'd made love and he lay sated beside her. She stroked the angles of his face, his hard jaw and sensuous mouth. "I love you," she said, not whispering this time.

He closed his eyes, and she wasn't sure if he was savoring her words or steeling himself against them.

She held her breath, waiting, again.

He tucked her head beneath his chest. "Such an angel," he said.

She felt his heart pound against her ear, but heard no other words, and she quickly realized this was an evasion. He didn't want to tell her that he didn't love her.

Her heart hurt so much she feared it would explode. She had made a huge mistake by being honest with Michael, but she didn't know how she could go back.

After the tenth day of Michael leaving early for work and returning late, Bella could no longer avoid the truth. She had changed things by telling him she loved him. She couldn't go back, and Michael could only pretend so much. She couldn't stand the idea that he wanted to avoid her.

She felt a combination of humiliation and disappointment with a dash of abandonment. *Oh, quit being a baby,* she told herself as she rose from his bed long after he'd left. She stroked the pillow where he'd slept, dipping her nose to breathe in his scent. She'd messed up.

She should have kept her mouth shut. She never should have admitted that she loved him.

Michael didn't know how to handle that. He didn't understand the concept of love. He'd grown up needing and wanting, but not getting. Now it was too late for him to truly receive. He couldn't bear her words or the deep emotion they conveyed. She'd shattered the fragile balance of their relationship.

Accepting the reality was painful. She wandered around his home, sensing this was her last time in his domain. Her stomach clenching so hard she could barely stand it, she wrote a note and left it on his pillow.

Her leaving would provide relief. More than anything, she just wanted his peace.

Michael came home on Tuesday night excited beyond belief. He couldn't wait to share his news with Bella. Possibilities bloomed in his mind. "Bella," he called. "Bella, I have news."

Silence greeted him. Maybe she was working late. Damn, he'd wanted to share this with her. He wandered upstairs to change his clothes. He pulled off his suit and stepped into jeans and a long-sleeve sweater to ward off the chill of the evening. Bella would make him warm later on, he thought, smiling to himself.

His glance strayed to the bed and he caught sight of a piece of paper on his pillow. Curious, he walked to the bed and picked up the folded paper. Unfolding it, he read it.

Dear Michael, I am so very sorry, but I cannot continue our affair. I have fallen in love with you. I know it's not what you want. It's messy and emotional and I don't know how to deal with it. I thought I knew what love was before I met you, but I was wrong. Now I just want you to be happy. If I leave, you won't feel pressured to do anything more than you want. I'll pay you back even if it takes my whole life. I promise. I wish you every good thing. Love, Bella.

Michael sucked in a quick, sharp breath. Bella was gone. He felt as if a knife had stabbed him between his ribs. She loved him and he couldn't love her back. How could he explain that he'd spent his life protecting himself so he wouldn't be hurt again? How could he explain that being self-sufficient was the only thing that had made him survive?

Loving meant being vulnerable, and he couldn't do that. For anyone.

Michael avoided his bed as long as possible and finally faced it without Bella's loving arms. How could he possibly sleep? he thought, tossing and turning. Hours later, he finally fell into a restless sleep where he dreamed of Bella. Her smile, her eyes, her touch. His alarm sounded and his arms were empty. No Bella. No joy.

He rose and worked out anyway.

"Don't ask," Bella said to her aunt as Charlotte looked at her with concern.

"How can I not?" Charlotte asked. "You have circles under your eyes. Your smile is a grimace."

"I just have to soldier through," Bella said. "It's one day at a time right now. Okay," she amended. "One hour at a time. It will get better. It will just take time."

"What happened?" Charlotte asked.

"I don't want to talk about it," Bella said.

Charlotte sighed. "Well, I realize this is horrible timing, but Fred and I have decided to get married."

Bella blinked in amazement. "You're going through with it?"

"Yeah," Charlotte said. "He says he can deal with anything that happens, even a recurrence of my cancer."

Bella smiled despite her own pain. "What a man."

"Yeah," Charlotte agreed. "What a man. We're going to do it in two weeks."

"So soon?" Bella said.

"When you get to be our age you don't want to waste time. We're going to go to the justice of the peace then have a party at my house. Would you be a witness?"

"Of course," Bella said, and hugged her aunt. "I'm so happy for you. You deserve this."

"Thank you, sweetie. Your time will come. I know it will," Charlotte said, but Bella had given up on Michael.

Bella had finally realized that to be willing to surrender to love was to be strong. She deserved to be loved.

Michael's cell phone vibrated as he reviewed the balance sheet for one of his restaurants. He glanced at the caller ID and picked up. "Hey, Rafe, what's up?"

"I'm in town," his brother said. "Feed me an early dinner."

Michael glanced at his watch. "It's three o'clock now. Are you going back tonight?"

"Yeah," Rafe said. "Now that I have Nicole and Joel, I don't like being away overnight if I can help it."

"Big switch for you," Michael said.

"Yes and a good one," he said. "So where do you want me to meet you?"

Michael was tempted to get a rain check. He hadn't been in a social mood since Bella had left. But Rafe *was* his brother, and after all they'd been through, he couldn't brush him aside.

"What are you in the mood for? Steak, Asian, seafood?"

"I'd like a good greasy burger and fries," he said.

"You got it. Meet me at Benson's downtown. See you in a few," he said, and hung up.

A half hour later, he and his brother sat in the bar of one of Michael's popular downtown restaurants. The server took their order as soon as they sat down.

Rafe grinned in approval. "One of the things I like

about eating with you is how great the service is. There's never a wait."

"I doubt you do much waiting wherever you go," Michael said.

Rafe shrugged and studied Michael. "Hey, are you okay? You look a little rough around the edges."

"Thanks, bro," Michael said wryly. "I've been working a lot lately."

"Yeah, well take a break every now and then. Even us Medicis have to do that."

"When I get a chance," Michael said and changed the subject. "How is Nicole?"

"Morning sickness appears to have hit except for her the nausea is worse in the evening. She can't stand the smell or sight of any kind of meat."

Michael nodded. "That's why you wanted a greasy burger."

"Yeah, this may be my only chance for a while. But I'm not complaining. She's worth it," Rafe said. "And this time, I'll be with her and the baby from the beginning."

Michael knew that Rafe still suffered from not knowing he'd had a child for the first three years of Joel's life. "It looks like you and Joel are getting along pretty well."

"Oh, yeah. He's a great kid. Nicole has done an amazing job with him. She sends her best, by the way, and still wants the recipe for that cake Bella made. You don't mind passing that on for me, do you?" Rafe asked as the waiter served their meal.

Michael had suspected the subject of Bella might come up, but he'd hoped it would happen nearer the end of the meal. His appetite suddenly disappeared. "That might be tough. Bella and I aren't seeing each other anymore."

Rafe blinked in surprise. "Really? I thought she must be important if you were introducing her to us. But I guess it's easy come, easy go."

"I wouldn't go that far," Michael muttered and took a drink of water.

Rafe frowned as he bit into his burger. "I don't understand. Are you saying she dumped you?"

"I didn't say that," Michael said. "She just wanted something I couldn't give her."

"Hmm," Rafe said and continued to eat his meal. "This is a great burger, by the way. I haven't had one in a week. So what did Bella want? A house in the South of France?"

Michael shook his head. "No. It wasn't anything like that. Nothing material. She just wanted me to have feelings for her that I'm not capable of."

"Oh," Rafe said. "You mean love."

Michael felt as if his brother had pointed a gun at his heart. "Yeah. I told her at the beginning, but things changed."

"You don't look too happy about it," Rafe said.

"I'm not, but there's nothing I can do about it."

"Do you love her?"

"I don't believe in love for myself. For other people, it's fine. It's not for me."

"Chicken," Rafe said in a matter-of-fact voice and lifted his hand before Michael could reply. "Hey, I was there, too. You think Damien wasn't? With our background, we keep our hearts under lock and key. Too much damage already done. Don't want to lose anymore. Trouble is, if you don't let the right one into the vault, you lose even more."

Michael couldn't listen to his brother's advice right now. He was still miserable about losing Bella. "Okay, thanks for the lecture. Can we change the subject?"

"Sure," Rafe said. "But it won't change that wretched feeling of loss in your gut."

"Thanks again," Michael said. "How's the yacht business?"

He listened to the news of Rafe's latest business ventures and shared some of his.

"Have you gotten any more news from your P.I. about Leo?"

"Just what I told you last week. What a roller-coaster ride. Last week, the PI tells me maybe he's alive but it will take longer to find him." He shook his head. "I don't know what to make of it."

"Me, either," Rafe said.

"I'm not giving up," Michael said.

"I wouldn't expect you to give up," Rafe said. "I need to go," Rafe said, rising. "Thanks for the meal. That burger was better than gourmet food for me."

"Glad I could do it," Michael said, joining his brother as he made his way to the door. "Tell Nicole to hang in there and give Joel a hug."

"Will do," Rafe said, then paused. "If you're this unhappy over Bella being gone, you might want to rethink your anti-love theory."

Michael shook his head. "No."

"Well, it looks to me like that ship has sailed. Maybe you've already fallen in love." Rafe lifted his hand and squeezed his shoulder. "Call me if you need me."

Two weeks later, Bella drove to the courthouse for Charlotte's wedding. Her aunt—dressed in an ivory and red silk suit and top—paced just outside the office of the justice of the peace.

"Are you okay?" Bella asked.

"Yeah, just a little edgy," Charlotte said. "Do you think I'm making a big mistake?"

"Do you love him?" Bella asked.

"Yes."

"Does he make you happy?" Bella asked.

Charlotte's expression softened. "Oh, yeah."

"I think you've answered your own question," Bella said, still devastated from her breakup with Michael.

"Okay," Charlotte said, glancing at her watch. "I think it's time."

Bella walked inside the office with her aunt. She looked up to find Michael standing beside Fred. She flashed a look of desperation at her aunt.

Charlotte mouthed the word *sorry* and turned her attention to her groom. Bella took a deep breath and focused on Charlotte. She absolutely couldn't think about Michael.

After Charlotte and her groom made their vows, the justice of the peace pronounced them husband and wife. Bella couldn't keep tears from her eyes.

"We'll see you at the house," Charlotte said then lowered her voice and kissed Bella. "Don't be too mad at me."

Charlotte and her new husband swept out of the courthouse, leaving Bella to face Michael.

"They look happy," Michael said.

"Yes, they do," she said, not wanting to meet his gaze. "I hope they will always be happy." She bit her lip. "I should leave. They're having a reception at Charlotte's house."

"Bella," he said, his voice causing her to stop in her tracks. "Charlotte called and told me you would be here."

She bit her lip again, not knowing what to say.

"You told me you loved me," he said.

She cringed because he hadn't been able to return her love.

"I don't know much about love," he said. "I gave up on it at an early age in order to survive."

She took a deep breath. "I can understand that."

"You've taught me something different," he said. "You've taught me that I'm capable of more than I thought I was. I don't know much about love, Bella, but I know I want you with me forever." He lifted her chin so that she would look at him. "I want you to teach me about your way of love."

Bella felt as if her heart would burst with happiness. "Oh, Michael. You already know how to love. You've already shown me so much love."

"Maybe we need each other to find the way," he said.

"Maybe," she said hopefully.

"I love you," he said. "And I'm determined to love you more."

Her eyes filled with tears. "You are an amazing man, Michael Medici. I want to help make you happy."

"You already have, Bella. You already have."

Epilogue

Ten days later, after her Aunt Charlotte and new husband had returned from Michael's new house in Grand Cayman, Bella caught her first break in days. She'd been in charge of the shop during her aunt's honeymoon and was looking forward to a quiet night with Michael.

How things had changed during the last week. Michael had completely opened up to her about his brother Leo, and she, too was on the edge of her seat waiting to find out more from the P.I.

Michael had arranged for all her belongings to be moved to his house. She was ready to soak in the Jacuzzi. She just hoped she could talk him into joining her. He was picking her up from work. She saw his vehicle pull alongside the curb and hopped in.

"Finally, a break," she said and kissed him. "I have plans for you."

"Oh, really," he said, his lips lifting in a slight grin. "What kind of plans?"

"Wet, bubbly plans," she said.

"Hmm. Not a bubble bath," he said.

"Not the kind you're thinking of," he said. "I thought I'd take you to one of my restaurants."

She would have preferred to be alone with him, but she was with him. That was good enough. "Okay. How was your day?"

"Busy. Rafe called. I keep forgetting to tell you that Nicole wants that recipe."

"Give me her e-mail and consider it done," she said as he pulled into the nearly empty parking lot of his restaurant. "Wow, I wonder what's going on. I've never seen the parking lot this empty at this time of night."

"I'll have to talk to the manager about that," he said and helped her from the car.

They walked to the door where a sign was posted. Private Event. Please return tomorrow.

"What's this?" she asked, confused.

He pushed open the door, and seemed much more calm than she would have expected. "We'll find out."

The lights were low and Michael led her to the bar where a bottle of champagne and two glasses sat on a table with two chairs.

She shot him a curious glance. "You knew about this. What's going on?"

"Have a seat. Let me pour your champagne," he said with a mysterious smile on his face.

He poured the bubbly and sat beside her. "Do you know what I like about this place?"

"Besides the fact that it's profitable?" she asked.

He chuckled. "Besides that."

"The good food. The atmosphere. The staff?" she asked, trying to gauge his mood. She'd never seen him like this before.

"I like this place because this is where I first saw you."

Her heart turned over and a lump formed in her throat. "I don't think you could touch me more deeply."

"I'm a high achiever. I'm not done yet," he said.

"What do you mean?"

"I mean that meeting you has changed me in ways I didn't dare dream. You were a wish I didn't even know I was making. I never believed in love until you."

Tears burned Bella's eyes. "Oh, Michael, you mean the same to me. I so want you to be happy."

"Then wear this," he said, pulling a black box from his pocket and opening it to reveal a sparkling diamond. "Wear this and marry me," he said. "I love you."

Bella shook her head in amazement. "Are you sure? Are you really sure?"

"I've spent my life figuring out the odds of winning and losing. I've never been more sure of something or someone in my life. There's no losing for me as long as I have you."

"I love you," she said. "I love you today, tomorrow and forever."

* * * * *

Don't miss SECRETS OF THE PLAYBOY'S BRIDE,
the next MEDICI MEN romance from
USA TODAY bestselling author Leanne Banks.
On sale March 9, 2010
from Silhouette Desire.

*Rancher Ramsey Westmoreland's temporary cook
is way too attractive for his liking.
Little does he know Chloe Burton came to his ranch
with another agenda entirely....*

That man across the street had to be, without a doubt, the most handsome man she'd ever seen.

Chloe Burton's pulse beat rhythmically as he stopped to talk to another man in front of a feed store. He was tall, dark and every inch of sexy—from his Stetson to the well-worn leather boots on his feet. And from the way his jeans and Western shirt fit his broad muscular shoulders, it was quite obvious he had everything it took to separate the men from the boys. The combination was enough to corrupt any woman's mind and had her weakening even from a distance. Her body felt flushed. It was hot. Unsettled.

Over the past year the only male who had gotten her time and attention had been the e-mail. That was simply pathetic, especially since now she was practically drooling simply at the sight of a man. Even his stance—both hands in his jeans pockets, legs braced apart, was a pose she would carry to her dreams.

And he was smiling, evidently enjoying the conversation being exchanged. He had dimples, incredibly sexy dimples in not one but both cheeks.

"What are you staring at, Clo?"

Chloe nearly jumped. She'd forgotten she had a lunch date. She glanced over the table at her best friend from college, Lucia Conyers.

"Take a look at that man across the street in the blue shirt, Lucia. Will he not be perfect for Denver's first issue of *Simply Irresistible* or what?" Chloe asked with so much excitement she almost couldn't stand it.

She was the owner of *Simply Irresistible*, a magazine for today's up-and-coming woman. Their once-a-year Irresistible Man cover, which highlighted a man the magazine felt deserved the honor, had increased sales enough for Chloe to open a Denver office.

When Lucia didn't say anything but kept staring, Chloe's smile widened. "Well?"

Lucia glanced across the booth at her. "Since you asked, I'll tell you what I see. One of the Westmorelands—Ramsey Westmoreland. And yes, he'd be perfect for the cover, but he won't do it."

Chloe raised a brow. "He'd get paid for his services, of course."

Lucia laughed and shook her head. "Getting paid won't be the issue, Clo—Ramsey is one of the wealthiest sheep ranchers in this part of Colorado. But everyone knows what a private person he is. Trust me—he won't do it."

Chloe couldn't help but smile. The man was the epitome of what she was looking for in a magazine cover and she was determined that whatever it took, he would be it.

"Umm, I don't like that look on your face, Chloe. I've seen it before and know exactly what it means."

She watched as Ramsey Westmoreland entered the store with a swagger that made her almost breathless. She *would* be seeing him again.

Look for Silhouette Desire's
HOT WESTMORELAND NIGHTS
by Brenda Jackson,
available March 9 wherever books are sold.

HARLEQUIN *Presents*

Self-Made
MILLIONAIRES

Devastating, dark-hearted and...
looking for brides.

Look for

BOUGHT:
DESTITUTE YET DEFIANT

by *Sarah Morgan*

#2902

From the lowliest slums to Millionaire's Row...
these men have everything now but their brides—
and they'll settle for nothing less than the best!

Available March 2010
from Harlequin Presents!

www.eHarlequin.com

HP12902

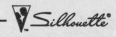

SPECIAL EDITION

FROM *USA TODAY* BESTSELLING AUTHOR
CHRISTINE RIMMER

A BRIDE FOR JERICHO BRAVO

Marnie Jones had long ago buried her wild-child
impulses and opted to be "safe," romantically
speaking. But one look at born rebel Jericho Bravo
and she began to wonder if her thrill-seeking side
was about to be revived. Because if ever there was
a man worth taking a chance on, there he was,
right within her grasp....

*Available in March
wherever books are sold.*

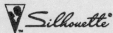

REQUEST YOUR FREE BOOKS!

**2 FREE NOVELS
PLUS 2
FREE GIFTS!**

Passionate, Powerful, Provocative!

YES! Please send me 2 FREE Silhouette Desire® novels and my 2 FREE gifts (gifts are worth about $10). After receiving them, if I don't wish to receive any more books, I can return the shipping statement marked "cancel." If I don't cancel, I will receive 6 brand-new novels every month and be billed just $4.05 per book in the U.S. or $4.74 per book in Canada. That's a saving of almost 15% off the cover price! It's quite a bargain! Shipping and handling is just 50¢ per book in the U.S. and 75¢ per book in Canada.* I understand that accepting the 2 free books and gifts places me under no obligation to buy anything. I can always return a shipment and cancel at any time. Even if I never buy another book, the two free books and gifts are mine to keep forever.

225 SDN E39X 326 SDN E4AA

Name	(PLEASE PRINT)	
Address		Apt. #
City	State/Prov.	Zip/Postal Code

Signature (if under 18, a parent or guardian must sign)

Mail to the **Silhouette Reader Service:**
IN U.S.A.: P.O. Box 1867, Buffalo, NY 14240-1867
IN CANADA: P.O. Box 609, Fort Erie, Ontario L2A 5X3

Not valid for current subscribers to Silhouette Desire books.

**Want to try two free books from another line?
Call 1-800-873-8635 or visit www.morefreebooks.com.**

* Terms and prices subject to change without notice. Prices do not include applicable taxes. N.Y. residents add applicable sales tax. Canadian residents will be charged applicable provincial taxes and GST. Offer not valid in Quebec. This offer is limited to one order per household. All orders subject to approval. Credit or debit balances in a customer's account(s) may be offset by any other outstanding balance owed by or to the customer. Please allow 4 to 6 weeks for delivery. Offer available while quantities last.

Your Privacy: Silhouette Books is committed to protecting your privacy. Our Privacy Policy is available online at www.eHarlequin.com or upon request from the Reader Service. From time to time we make our lists of customers available to reputable third parties who may have a product or service of interest to you. If you would prefer we not share your name and address, please check here. ☐

Help us get it right—We strive for accurate, respectful and relevant communications. To clarify or modify your communication preferences, visit us at www.ReaderService.com/consumerchoice.

SDES10